PINING FOR THE PHOTOGRAPHER

DEBBIE WHITE

PINING FOR THE PHOTOGRAPHER

BY
Debbie White

Copyright © 2019 by Debbie White

All Rights Reserved

Editing by Kerry Genova, writersresourceinc.com

Emily drove her badly scratched and dented Outback to a rural countryside road where the summer heat and rain-deprived long days turned the wispy fields a deep yellow. A wood and wire fence ran along the property, and the dry hills served as a backdrop. She drove a bit more before turning off to a place that was well-known for photo shoots. People found the most obscure places for photos. She lifted her little companion, Daisy, a blue merle Pembroke Welsh corgi into her arms, gathered her things, and exited the car.

A young couple with their eyes closed and smooching made her smile. They were oblivious to her approaching.

"Ahem."

The young blonde giggled. "Oh, hey. I'm Jessica." She flopped up her hand in a wave.

"I'm Clark. And you must be Emily." He reached for her hand.

"What gave it away? The camera?" She drew her gaze from him and landed them on Jessica, then laughed.

"I guess so," he said with a chuckle.

"Let me get set up. I think this is a beautiful place for a picture. I've been out here a few times." She pulled open the tripod and set her camera in place.

"You mean we aren't the first ones to discover this?" Jessica pulled out her bottom lip and pouted.

Emily had her eye in the lens, trying to focus her camera. She raised her head slowly. "Seriously?"

"We thought it was something special just for us." Clark pulled his girl close, giving her a peck on the forehead.

"It'll be special for you because it will have you both in it," Emily spoke in a humorless style. Shaking her head, she lowered her gaze back to the camera lens and began to touch buttons, causing the camera to make clicking sounds. Emily could hear rumblings coming from the happy, soon-to-be-married couple. When she looked up, a gun was pointing at her. She gulped.

She suddenly had a flashback to the couple who insisted on dressing like the farmer and wife with a pitchfork resembling the American Gothic painting, and the time another couple wanted their picture to have their potbellied pig in it or the couple who dressed like wannabe bikers. The scary kind. And there were many more she absolutely refused to even take. Sometimes you can't unsee stuff. But she had to admit, this was a first. "Oh, this is a strange sort of prop. But whatever you all want." Her gaze darted from the guy to the girl and back to him, holding the gun.

"This isn't a prop," the girl said, her giggly tone suddenly becoming brazen.

Emily stumbled away from the tripod. "What's going on here?"

The guy with the gun, who Emily thought was some nimble-head getting engaged, stepped toward her. She drew her head back and narrowed her eyes.

"We heard you got a lot of money."

Emily peered at them through half-closed lids. She swallowed down the lump in her throat and clasped her hands. "Who told you that?"

The guy nodded over to his accomplice.

"I work at the bank," the young woman said, smirking.

It was true. Emily had inherited a boatload of money from her late grandmother. She'd had it all transferred over into various accounts while she figured out what to do with it. If she made it out of this situation alive, she'd open a studio. The heck with doing remote shoots. But she'd been looking for a reasonable place to rent, and with the sky-high cost of real estate in Los Angeles, she couldn't find anything in her budget.

"You know you won't get away with this. Kidnapping and extortion hold serious penalties. It's not worth it. If you get in your car and drive away, everything will be okay."

"That's not going to happen, lady," Jessica, the fake soon-to-be bride said.

Clark held the gun a few inches from her. "You're going to drive to the bank and take out some money. Not all of it, but enough for us to start a new life with. From what I understand, you have plenty. Jessica will follow us in your car." His gaze dropped down to Daisy. "Your mutt stays here, though."

"No, please don't. That's a very cruel thing to do. Daisy

wouldn't survive a few hours out in this heat without water. Not to mention the wild animals. Please let me take her with me. She won't be any problem at all. I promise."

Clark hunched his shoulders. Emily watched the two as they decided her fate. She tried to think fast. This situation was not good. She slowly reached her hand and rested it on her pocket. Her cell phone was there. If she could somehow mash a button, maybe someone could hear what was going on.

"Keep your hands where I can see them," Clark blurted.

Emily slowly opened her hands to show him they were empty. "Sorry."

"Let's go, Clark. I have to go to the bathroom," Jessica wailed, her whiny, girly voice coming back into play.

Emily sized up Jessica. She could probably take her. Although she'd always been taught it wasn't nice to fight. But Clark and the gun. That would be another issue. But now was the time to see if all her lessons paid off. In one swift movement, she straightened out her leg, and with as much force, she kicked Clark in the groin. When he went down, the gun fell out of his grip. Emily quickly picked it up and pointed it at them. But as Clark staggered to his feet, Daisy grabbed hold of his pant leg and began shaking her head wildly with the cloth clenched tightly between her teeth. Clark screamed. "Get your dog off of me."

Emily watched on as Jessica cried, and Clark yelled in pain from the kick to his soft spot and Daisy chewing on him madly. She called 9-1-1 and thankful she had cell service, waited for the police to arrive.

Shaken but still focused, Emily gave her statement to the police. She observed as the handcuffed couple was taken into custody. After all the excitement, she needed a drink. She gathered her photography equipment and Daisy and headed to a local watering hole for a margarita and basket of chips and salsa. Her best friend Kayla said she'd be there waiting for them.

She looked in the rearview mirror and saw the billows of dust as the two police cruisers tore off down the road. Shaking her head, she started the engine. "I sure hope those guys don't expect their deposit back."

SHE PLOPPED down onto the black metal chair and clipped Daisy's leash onto one of the table legs. She curled up like a donut and rested after an exciting day.

"I can't believe those idiots. Did they really think they were going to get away with such a dumb crime?" Kayla said.

Kayla and Emily had been friends for several years. After Emily first moved to L.A., Kayla was the first person she met. They rented studio apartments at the same complex. They hit it off, the girl from Chicago with long brown hair and big blue eyes, and the petite, olive complexioned dark beauty from Texas.

"I knew it wouldn't bode well if I got into the car with them. I decided to see how much of my martial arts training paid off. I kept thinking about what the instructor told us over and over. Hit him where it counts. Find any soft spot and take him down."

"Well, I'm glad it worked out. And Daisy, she's quite the guard dog," Kayla said, looking under the table at a softly snoring corgi, watching as the little ball of fluff's chest rose and fell.

"You should have seen her. She latched onto him and wasn't going to let go. I'm so proud of her."

Over a shared plate of sizzling fajitas, the girls talked about everything from who Kayla was dating now, to her new job as an assistant to a well-known actor. Seemed everyone either worked for a famous person or was trying to break into acting themselves. Kayla was a drama queen, but she didn't have as much desire to be an actress as to be surrounded by them. She got it naturally. Her brother, Connor, was an actor. Mostly stage productions. He lived in New York. Emily met him when Kayla and she did a tour of the city and had front row seats to his play. After, he took them to some splashy restaurant where they got to meet some of the other actors. Most of them weren't as well known as the Hollywood types, but it was fun all the same.

"Guess who's coming to California?" Her blue eyes sparkled.

Emily furrowed her brows. Talk about a shot in the dark. "I don't know, who?"

"My brother, Connor."

Emily raised her gaze and focused on Kayla. "That's great. How long is he staying for?"

She recalled how cute he was. Medium brown hair, blue eyes like Kayla, tall, well-built, and a few freckles here and there giving him the boy next door look. She moistened her dry mouth with a sip of her margarita.

"He has an audition. For a movie," Kayla yelled out. "In fact, two movies!"

A few heads turned their way.

"Sorry. I'm excited for him."

"You should be. That's wonderful. Was this audition something you helped pave the way for with your connections?"

"No, actually someone sat in on the last night of his performance and met him backstage. Said they had a perfect part for him. He's always dreamed of making it out here, so now is his chance." Her smile beamed across the outdoor seating area.

"Well, I wish him a lot of luck. I need to really focus on finding a studio. I'm not going out to those faraway shoots anymore. I want to have plenty of backdrops so I can give all my clients a feel of outdoors, or whatever it is they're looking for."

"I don't blame you at all. This world is a crazy place."

Emily cocked her head, then laughed. Something about those words sparked humor. Probably because Kayla was only thirty years old. What on earth could she compare this world to? "I'm starting tomorrow on my hunt. I'll let you know what I find out."

Then the aroma of a sizzling plate of beef and chicken strips with green peppers and onion wafted to their table. The server set down a small container of tortillas, and a divided dish with guacamole, sour cream, and salsa. "Enjoy," he said, backing away.

Emily dipped her fork into the platter and pulled out some meat and tossed it into her flour tortilla. She topped it with guacamole and a dab of sour cream and bit into it. "Oh, man. This is so good," she said as she chewed, her cheeks puffed out like a squirrel hoarding nuts.

"Oh, by the way, I told Connor we'd go out with him

and paint the town red." Kayla bit into her own stuffed tortilla.

Emily almost choked on her food. She quickly swallowed down the stuck piece of tortilla with a sip from her drink. How had Kayla known she'd like nothing more than to see his handsome face again?

<h1 style="text-align:center">CHAPTER 2</h1>

Kayla jumped up from her seat and began patting Emily on the back. "Are you all right?" She gave her one last touch of her hand.

"Yes, I'm fine." She grinned sheepishly.

"Okay, 'cuz you sort of scared me when your eyes rolled into the back of your head." Kayla sat back down.

Emily leaned over and ran her hand across Daisy's back. "I was surprised by your news of your brother."

Kayla flashed her a broad smile. "I thought there was a bit of a spark between you two." She picked up her glass and slurped the lime-flavored drink through a straw, then wiped the salt from the rim and licked it.

"Spark? Who? Us?" Emily could feel the rush of warmth spread across her face.

Kayla gave her best impression of Scarlet O'Hara. "I know he's good-looking. I hear it from all of my coworkers. They'd love to have a date with him." She fanned her face, pretending it was burning up with desire.

Emily chortled. "Whatever."

9

"Please. You know you two like each other."

"Kayla, it's been over a year since I saw him. There was a slight attraction. And I'm emphasizing slight."

"He thought you were pretty cute," Kayla said.

"I don't know how he could have thought anything after just one dinner out," Emily said, shielding her lying eyes.

"Wasn't it more like a dinner and a breakfast?" Kayla shrugged, the corners of her mouth drawing up at the same time.

Emily sighed. "All right. I'll paint the town red with you guys. No worries. I'm in. I'm all in." Emily took another bite of her stuffed tortilla and chewed.

AFTER LUNCH and a whole lot of ribbing from her best friend, Emily headed back to her apartment with Daisy. It'd been one eventful day between having a gun pulled on her, to doing some krav maga moves on her assailant and finishing it up with news of Connor Stone coming to town. She tossed her worn-out body across her bed and closed her eyes. Daisy ruffled up her blanket before settling on her bed, and the two tired souls began snoring softly before long.

She couldn't have been asleep long before her phone began to play "Cruise" by Florida Georgia Line.

"Hello," she said, her voice cracking.

She sat up, wiping her eyes. "Yes, this is she."

"I'm calling because you left a message regarding the loft space for rent. When do you want to see it?"

Emily cleared her throat. "I can be over there in about forty-five minutes."

She quickly freshened up by splashing water on her face and running a brush through her hair. She pulled it back in a rubber band, not wanting to take the time to style it. She spritzed on some perfume, moistened her lips with some shiny lip gloss and hitched Daisy up to her leash. All the while driving through horrific L.A. traffic, weaving in and out of cars, Emily dreamed of her new studio and how proud her late grandmother would be. She also heard in the background her dad saying don't put the cart before the horse. She smirked.

She'd looked away for a second when, bam! "Gah!" She held her foot firmly on the brake while holding Daisy from flying off the seat. Her heart beating a mile a minute, she put the old car in gear and sighed. "Not today," she said out loud.

The two cars made their way to the shoulder. Not an easy task in commute traffic in L.A. They both sat for a few seconds before getting out of their cars.

"I'm sorry. I got distracted." Emily shrugged.

"The guy in front me sort of stopped quick," the young man of about seventeen said.

"Let's exchange insurance information. I'll give you my number. No need to call the cops, right?" the young man said, clearly nervous.

"Is this your parents' car?" Emily asked.

He nodded.

"Well, I don't see any real damage to my car, and there's only a little paint from my car on your bumper." She smiled.

"Great. I'm good then. Thanks." He trotted off toward his car.

"Now, don't mistake this sign of kindness as a sign of weakness. Don't come back and say I left the scene or anything," Emily yelled.

He gave her a wave. "No worries," he called out. Then he shut the door and drove off quickly.

"Please don't make me regret this," she said, getting into her car. She checked her mirrors and merged with traffic. Because of this little incident, she would be late for her appointment. She gave the car a little more gas and soared down the freeway.

"I'M sorry I'm late. I had a little fender bender on the way here." Emily extended her hand. "Emily King."

"I was getting ready to lock up and head out. A phone call would have been nice." His gaze lowered to Daisy.

"Yes, I apologize. This is my little dog, Daisy."

"I see." His clear disdain for dogs showed.

Emily frowned at the little old man when he turned his back.

"My client wants a quick lease. Are you ready to act on something fast?" He raised his brows.

"If it fits my needs. Of course." She wandered around the large, empty space.

"It's about twenty-four-hundred square feet of space," the agent said.

"I love the exposed ceilings. The large windows are great for what I'd use it for." She crossed over to a wall where an opening was. She poked her head inside. "Oh, nice."

"Yes, a full kitchen and bathroom. This is both a commercial and residential space. What did you say you were going to do with it?"

"A photography studio."

"Oh. Do you plan to use it as a work and live situation?"

"No, just work."

"Would your client be interested in selling it versus leasing it?" Emily batted her lashes a few times. She didn't like to pull the flirty girl look, but sometimes it worked.

"I don't know. She's always leased it before. But I guess I could float the idea. You do realize it will be very expensive. The close proximity to Hollywood and all." He tipped his head, then ran his hand along his chin. "I can ask, and I'll get back to you. But if not, are you interested in leasing?"

"Either way."

INSTEAD OF GOING STRAIGHT HOME, she stopped at the local market to get yogurt and fresh fruit. After a heavy lunch, she'd be eating light. She tossed in some of the gourmet canned dog food for Daisy, a few more items on her list and headed for check out.

Daisy sat in the grocery cart like the prima donna she was, letting people pet her, talk baby-talk to her and rub her under her chin. Emily giggled. After they paid, they put the cart up, Emily lifted Daisy from the cart and set her down, and grabbed her bag of groceries. She looked both ways then headed for the car. Juggling the bag, Daisy's leash, and the key fob, her phone began to ring. She quickly identified the number, answering it with a breathy hello.

"Emily King?"

"Yes."

"I spoke with my client. She's not interested in selling the property at this time. However, she said she'd keep it under advisement, and if in the future she decides, she'll consider giving you first opportunity. Do you still want to lease it?"

"I told you today. Either way. I want it."

"Good. Can you stop by my office to sign the agreement and pick up the keys?"

Emily smiled all the way to his office. Finally, a studio of her own.

SIGNING the lease agreement never felt so good to Emily. She had to pinch herself to believe it. She got the okay to paint the inside, put up some temporary partitions and set out to order backdrops, portable lighting, and took some of her favorite photos and framed them to display.

Little Daisy, who couldn't keep her eyelids open any longer, trotted off to bed, leaving Emily at the table to burn the midnight oil. She snapped shut her laptop and stretched. Soon a long yawn escaped her lips. She'd completed her list of tasks. All equipment and furniture ordered. Thank goodness for the internet and home delivery. She'd be up and running in no time.

She rinsed out the cup that held her sleepytime tea,

turned off the lights, and padded off to bed. She vaguely recalled getting in under the covers. When she opened her eyes, sunshine peeked through her blinds, gently waving to her, letting her know she'd overslept.

She rubbed the sleep from her eyes and yawned. She rolled over and locked eyes with Daisy. "Good morning, baby girl."

After feeding Daisy, she poured her freshly brewed coffee in a tall thermal cup, leashed Daisy up and headed to the nearby park. It would be a quick jaunt. She had a full day of photo shoots.

Her first appointment was with another diva of sorts, and Daisy loved the attention Lorna Douglas gave her, not to mention the gourmet treats by a Hollywood dog baker. Daisy, with her full tummy, lay with her legs out in the true sploot fashion of a content pup and watched with careful eyes as Emily positioned Ms. Douglas, ensuring the light caught her lovely complexion. She fluffed up her hair and brought it forward, draping it over her shoulders, then she tilted her head up and to the right a tad.

"Hold that," she said, stepping back and clicking away.

She set the camera on the tripod and crossed over to the other side of Ms. Douglas's living room, checking the light and ambience.

"Do you have another room we could do a photo in?"

"My bedroom?" She raised her brows to her hairline.

Ms. Douglas led Emily to the room in question. "Maybe over there." She pointed to the large bay window where two upholstered chairs with a table between them sat. A vase of colorful flowers sat on the table.

"Let's try it."

The movie star of many box-office hits took possession of one of the chairs and posed. Getting her picture taken was not something new to her. However, this was personal. She was getting ahead of the crowds for holiday cards. Every year she did a Christmas card with herself as the image. Decked out in all white, and now sitting in a gold brocade chair with red and gold drapes behind her, Emily was convinced this would be the perfect picture for her Christmas cards. She clicked away.

"How are you doing in your search for a studio?" Lorna asked.

"I signed a contract for a year's lease for a great studio near here. I can't wait to get settled in." Emily stayed focused and didn't look up. "I don't know if you heard about my little incident out on location."

"Everyone has heard about it. You know news such as that travels fast around here. I'm so glad you weren't hurt. What in the world were those imbeciles thinking?"

"I don't think they were giving anything much thought. That's the problem." Emily giggled.

"True. But how can you be assured some bad person doesn't stalk you at your new location?"

"Security. The building has lots of it. Besides, I plan to keep up my martial arts training. I never thought in a million years I'd use it. But it came in handy."

"I hear Daisy jumped in as well."

Emily peered over at the little dog who now was sleeping on her back with all paws up. "She held her own."

"Are we through?" Lorna Douglas stood, smoothing out her all-white attire.

"I think so. I'll get the proofs developed and deliver them in a few days." She peered at her phone. "But right now, we have to get going for our next gig."

Lorna embraced Emily in a strong hug. "Thank you, dear."

Emily's nose wrinkled when she took in the star's strong perfume. She gently pushed out of her arms. "No worries. We'll be in touch. Come on, Daisy."

Emily placed her equipment into the back of her car, put Daisy in the front seat, and off they sped to her next appointment. This one she wasn't looking forward to. The famous pop singer was constantly trying to make her one of his next conquests.

"Hello, Jake," she said as she set up the tripod. Daisy found a spot where the sun streaked through and lay down.

With his messy hair, five o'clock shadow, tall, lean build, and tats all up and down his arms, Jake was the bad boy of the industry. She'd read a lot about him. But boy could he belt out the love songs. And those bedroom eyes. Yeah, they could totally mess up some girl's head. But not hers. Nope. She had her head screwed on tight, and Jake couldn't try to persuade her to do anything no matter how hard he tried. And he tried.

"Are you still single, Emily King." He winked as he stood against a white wall with his hands dug deep into his jean pockets.

"Single and loving it." *A little lie surely couldn't hurt?*

"I could change all that, if you'd let me," he sang out with a low, gravelly tone.

"That's quite all right, Jake. I like being single. It means I don't have to answer to anyone. Besides, Daisy is pretty picky." She loved to throw Daisy in the conversation.

Jake narrowed his eyes and peered over to Daisy, who was curled up in a donut, sleeping away. "I like dogs."

"Yes, but she doesn't like you." She clicked a few frames.

"Come on, Emily. One date. That's all it takes to get hooked on old Jake." He ran his hand through his hair, admittedly sending some waves of excitement through her bones. She shook her head. "No, Jake. I mean it. Leave me alone."

"You don't know what you're missing," he said light-heartedly.

Tired of the serenading and pleading, she gasped. "Seriously, Jake. Stop it already. Now, where else do you want your picture taken?" She placed her hands on her hips.

He hung his head, staring at his boots. When he raised his head, he locked eyes with her. "You've hurt me, Emily." He patted his heart, feigning heartbreak.

"Whatever. You'll move on. Now, show me where you want the last set taken. I have another appointment today."

He led the way to the music room.

He picked up his guitar and placed the strap over his head. "How about this?"

"I think it will be perfect for the cover of your book."

After she took a few pictures of him with the guitar, they got one of him sitting behind the baby grand piano, then they wrapped it up.

"I'll have the proofs done in a few days and deliver them shortly."

"By the way, I heard what happened to you. You know, if you had me in your life that wouldn't have happened." He inched his way toward her.

"Oh?"

"I would have never let you out of my sight."

She could feel the warmth of his breath with each word spoken. She swallowed and blinked. "What makes you think I'd want a boyfriend like that anyway?"

"Because you need someone to take care of you, remind you how beautiful you are, and how special you are." His nose was a few inches from her. She licked her lips and stepped back. Daisy, awakened from her nap, growled. Jake turned toward her.

"What's her problem?"

"I told you earlier. She doesn't like you. And she's a pretty good judge of character. Come on, Daisy. Time to hit the road."

"Emily, don't do me like that," he cried.

She gave him a backhanded wave. "You'll survive, Jake. Onward and upward to your new conquest. She's around the bend somewhere." Emily giggled.

SHE PULLED into her final stop for the day. Still reeling from her episode with Jake, she felt a little flustered. She downed a bottled water before going in.

A little girl dressed in a white dress with a red sash opened the door. "Hi, Emily!"

"Hey, Joy. How are you?"

"Mommy. Emily is here."

Emily had been taking family portraits of the Wilson family since Joy was an infant. Now she was six years old. Born on Christmas Day, the Wilson's not only expected family pictures to calendar the event but looked forward to it as they used it for their Christmas card.

"Hi, Emily," Heather, Joy's mother, said.

"Are you all ready?"

"Ready as we'll ever be. We have a new addition to the family this year."

Emily furrowed her brows. She hadn't heard of Heather expecting. She still maintained her girly figure. Her eyes went to Heather's flat stomach.

Heather laughed. "No, not a human addition."

A chocolate Lab puppy with a red bow around its neck came galloping out of another room. Peter, Heather's husband, was trailing behind. The puppy ran up to Daisy, and they began to sniff each other. Daisy started wagging her tail, then the puppy started prancing all around her, and soon Daisy and Ryder began dancing the happy-dog dance.

"He's adorable," Emily said, patting him on the head.

Today was the day everyone seemed to be in white. Except for Jake. He wore tight blue jeans, and a dusty blue tee-shirt tucked into his slim-fitting jeans, a brown leather belt, and boots. Not that she noticed. She shook her head.

"Let's get started, shall we?"

"We heard what happened, Emily. I hope they throw the book at those creeps," Heather said through gritted teeth as she smiled for the camera.

"Me, too. I can't believe they thought they would get away with it," Peter said as he held Ryder steady.

It took skill to take pictures of children, but it took a lot more with animals. You had to be ready to hit that button fast. And Emily did.

Satisfied something would be suitable for their Christmas cards, Emily bid them goodbye and headed toward home. But not before a quick stop to her local Vietnamese restaurant for some delicious takeout.

As soon as she entered the small establishment, the owner, who she'd known for quite some time, wrapped her arms around her and gave her a hug. "I heard about the holdup. Are you okay?" She held her back and stared at her. Emily nodded. "Yes, I'm fine."

"Whatever you want. On the house."

"You're too kind, Sue, but I have money. They didn't get it."

"The usual?" she called out as she headed back to the kitchen.

"Yes, please."

The aroma from the Vietnamese specialty, a chicken chow mein with carrots, celery, cabbage, broccoli, and a house oyster sauce filled the interior of the car, making her tummy grumble with hunger and Daisy pant. It'd been a long day, and the idea of her legs curled up underneath her while eating her comfort food appealed to her more and more. She raced down the road toward her apartment.

While she dug into the white cartons containing noodles and other delicious items, she checked her email. Several notices of her recent purchases along with anticipated delivery dates consumed most of the mail. A note from her mom popped up too. She quickly scanned the message.

Hi, Emily!

Wondered if you were up for a visit anytime soon? Dad and I would love to see you and Daisy! Call me!

Love, Mom

Emily sat back in her chair partly to help her digest her food and somewhat to consider her mom's message. She continually insisted on doing things the old-school way. *Really? Sending me an email instead of picking up the phone.* The two-hour time difference might have something to do with it, or at least that's what she'll say. "I'll give her a call tomorrow morning."

A long, hot bubble bath was in order after the past couple of days. She drew the bath, dropped in one of the lavender-scented bath bombs Kayla gave her for Christmas, and made herself a cup of piping hot tea while the tub filled. The faucet screeched as she turned off the water. She slowly poked her toes in, testing the temperature. Satisfied she could take the heat, she eased her body into the sudsy water. Closing her eyes, she sank deeper into the warm bliss, resting her head on another Christmas present from Kayla, an inflatable bath pillow the shape of a seashell. "Ahh. This. This is so worth the past few days." She peered over to find Daisy resting her chin on her paws and blinking at her. "Mommy loves the baby girl," she sang. Daisy popped her head up and came over to the bathtub. Emily removed a soapy, drippy hand and gently patted Daisy's head. Daisy shook the bubbles away, turned around and made a *humph* sound as she dropped back down to the rug, this time closing her eyes.

Emily recalled when she got Daisy. Still a pup at the

age of twelve months, she was surrendered by her owner to an animal rescue because pups take a lot of time and corgis need attention. Emily had always been passionate about animal rescue. In fact, she donated money every year to the local shelter, so when one of her clients had shared Daisy's information with her, she decided the time might be right to get a dog of her own. One look into Daisy's heavenly eyes, she knew she had to adopt her. Emily's eyes filled with tears when she thought about the day Daisy came to live with her, but she also thought about the day she'd leave her. "Please make it be a lot of years from now," she said, looking at the ceiling.

CHAPTER 3

Moving day into the new studio was exciting for Emily. Daisy seemed a bit perturbed. She'd get comfortable in one spot and have to be rustled to another area. Finally, she trotted off to the back room and stayed there until every last delivery for the day had occurred. When Emily went searching for her, she found her curled up in a donut shape, fast asleep. She perked up when she heard Emily's voice.

"I know, baby girl. It's been another rough day. But come see." Emily folded her fingers, urging her to come.

Emily skipped through the large place and stood in front of a cushy dog bed. "Ta-da." She pointed to the bed. Daisy blinked a few times, then gingerly stepped onto the bed. "No more jostling. This is your bed while Mommy works." She dropped to her bottom and crossed her legs, scratching Daisy behind the ears and under her chin. A loud chiming noise startled them both.

"Intercom." She rose and crossed to the box on the wall near the door. She mashed a black button. "Yes?"

"Hi, Ms. King?"

"Yes?"

"There's a detective here to speak to you. I've checked his credentials. He appears to be on the up and up," Joe, the security guard said.

"Sure, I'll speak with him, Joe. Send him up."

"I love this security, wish I had it at my apartment. Maybe I should consider moving in here," she said, her eyes settling on Daisy. Daisy wagged her tail.

A knock at the heavy metal door jolted her. She made her way toward it, opening it wide for the detective.

He handed her a card while stepping inside the loft. "I understand you just moved in?"

"Yes, literally today."

"I was hoping you had a few minutes to talk to me about the incident involving Jessica Malcomb and Clark Smith."

"Sure. I don't really know much. They contacted me through my website and set up a photo shoot for their engagement. They picked the location, gave me a five-hundred-dollar deposit, and I drove out there."

"Had you been to that location before?" He took pen to paper while focusing on her.

"A few times. It's a place known for picture taking."

"So, none of that alarmed you?" He locked eyes with her.

"No, not until he pointed the gun at me. But even then, I wasn't quite sure until his partner changed personalities on me in a flash. Then I realized they weren't messing around. This was for real."

"Then what happened?"

"I did what my martial arts instructor has trained me

to do. I stayed focused and calm, and when the opportunity presented itself, I kicked him where he'd see stars. He dropped the gun, I kicked it out of his reach and picked it up, holding them until the cops came."

"And I guess you have a pit bull or something? Clark sustained some pretty bad bites."

"A pit bull?" Emily reared her head back and laughed. "Here's my pit." She pointed to Daisy.

"That's the dog that attacked him?" The detective's eyes grew wide.

"She loves her mommy. What can I say?" Emily shrugged.

"Do you have any treats? I'd like to give her one."

"Are you kidding? Corgis are notorious for a few things, and treats are one." Emily raced to the kitchen and retrieved a bag of Daisy's favorites.

Daisy quickly smelled the morsels and reared up on her back legs, with her front legs curled slightly. Her back was straight as a board.

"This is what I like to call sitting pretty." Emily handed the bag to the detective.

He dug inside and pulled out a tidbit and gave it to Daisy. Daisy munched it right away.

She uncurled and curled her front paws again as if to wave to the detective. But really it was more like pleading for more treats.

The detective pulled out another and tossed it to her mouth. Daisy chomped down quickly while balancing on her hind legs. When she realized she wouldn't get any more, she lowered to her meerkat position and waddled back over to her bed.

"Well, I think I've got everything I need to finish my

report." The detective stood, making his way toward the door.

"Are they still in jail?" Emily rested her hand on the black lever-style handle and slid it.

"Yes. They're not going anywhere for a long time. Don't you worry."

After the detective left, Emily finished setting up her studio so she could start taking clients. She made a few calls to see if those already on the schedule minded coming to her new place. Most were agreeable, especially after they learned what had happened. She only had two out of her ninety-day calendar insist on staying with their chosen place. She understood why they wanted some of the remote locations. And she had to realize not everyone would want the pictures taken in the studio every time.

IT WASN'T TOTALLY awful to have to leave the studio. On gorgeous days such as today, getting pulled outside was a blessing. Emily packed her beach bag with all the essentials. Doritos, bottled water, sunscreen lotion, Daisy's water dish, a couple of towels, a couple of glossy gossip magazines, and her camera. She hitched Daisy up to her leash and off they went.

The beach was crowded like most days when the sun was shining, and the temperature was hot. She found a small spot to lay out her towel and pitch her umbrella. But first, she had to dig a small hole in the sand to secure it. Once the shade was up, Daisy got comfortable and began to people watch. Emily laughed. She was so human-like it amazed her. Emily lathered on the sunscreen, exposing her back to the warmth first before turning over. She sat straight up.

"Hey. Sorry. I didn't mean to startle you."

Emily smiled. "No worries. What can I do for you?"

Daisy let out a growl.

"Daisy!" Emily tapped her on the nose. "Be good."

"She's being protective," the young man said.

"Anyway, is this yours?" He held out a magazine.

Emily reached for it, studying the cover. "Yes. It must have blown away when I wasn't paying attention."

"Enjoy the beach." The young man waved while stepping away from them.

"Sorry again about the dog. She really is a nice dog. Never bit anyone before. Well almost," she said, her voice trailing off when she recalled the gun incident.

The guy chuckled as he left.

"What's gotten into you, Daisy? Not every guy is a bad dude."

During the rest of their stay at the beach, Emily noticed that whenever a guy walked too close to them, Daisy stared at him through squinted lids and watched him every step of the way until he'd passed them. This was strange behavior for her. Shaking her head, Emily realized that maybe Daisy was experiencing some negative behavior as a result of the scary situation. She quickly dialed her vet.

"There's no doubt she's a bit skittish. She's typically laid-back. I think maybe she would benefit with help from an animal behaviorist." The vet turned and opened a nearby drawer, retrieving a card. "She's good. I've only heard great things about her."

Emily narrowed her eyes as she read the name on the card. "Okay. I'll give her a call."

"Let me know how it goes." The vet patted Emily on the shoulder.

Daisy let out a soft rumble.

"See what I mean." Emily lowered her head.

"I do. She's never done that before. Go see Lorraine."

Emily lifted Daisy off the chrome examining table and hooked her leash to her collar. She made her way past the waiting room filled with clients. Daisy stopped in front of one of the chairs where a young man sat. He smiled and began to reach for Daisy. She snapped and pulled away.

"Daisy!" Emily yelled.

The man smirked.

"I'm so sorry. She's going through some stuff. I'm trying to get her help."

Emily quickly exited the veterinarian office. Her heart beating a mile a minute, she began to cry. She couldn't have a dog that bit and reacted to people wanting to pet her. She had clients. The clients had children. Daisy used to love being around all the people. "That creep! He ruined my dog forever." She wailed in her cupped hands. Soon a wet, cold black nose wiggled between her fingers. "I'm sorry, girl. We'll get through this. I have to have faith." She cradled Daisy in her arms and kissed her repeatedly on the head.

EMILY MADE the appointment before she even pulled out of the parking lot, then she hurried back to the studio for her photo shoot.

Digging into her purse to find her key, Emily profusely apologized for her tardiness, unlocking the door and motioning for her clients to step inside.

"I'm so sorry I'm late. I had to take Daisy to the vet. Please give me a moment, and I'll get going." She led Daisy to the back room where she loaded her up on treats, patted her head, and gave her a look that whispered, "be good." She gently closed the door behind her and moved toward the center of the studio. The couple stood with hands laced, rocking back and forth and smiling while Emily set the camera up.

Checking over her notes, she refreshed her memory of why the couple was there. "So let's see, you want pictures today for your portfolio. Is that correct?"

The skinny young woman who probably was barely nineteen years old bobbed her head up and down. Emily's gaze drifted to the guy standing to her right. He was probably more like twenty, had a broad grin, fabulous teeth, and the boy next door look that many modeling agencies were looking for. She glanced back at the girl with the stringy hair and malnourished body and wondered what he saw in her. Surely, she had to know that he would make it big only to dump her. Wasn't that the way it went?

"Okay, so you want singles and a few of you together too?" Emily focused her camera without taking her eyes off her subjects.

"Yeah, that's would be awesome," the young man said.

Emily cleared her throat. "Okay, let me start with the singles." She read her notes. "Michael, why don't you stand over near the wood desk, and let's see if I can get some serious pictures of you."

She followed him over to the desk and began to position him. "Lean up here and turn your head this way," she said, positioning his limp limbs as if he were a doll.

She rolled up the cuffs of his blue button-down shirt and unbuttoned the top three, exposing his chest. Her gaze floated down his frame and back up to his eyes. She stepped back and eyed him one last time then went to the camera.

"Now let's try a few behind the desk."

Michael circled around the large piece of furniture and took a seat in the high-back desk chair.

"Clasp your hands out front and look straight at the camera." She rushed back to her camera and clicked away. Peering up, she gave him a few more commands. "Look to the right as if something has caught your attention. You have a great profile." She put her eyes to the lens and began to shoot the scene. "I think those will look great. Any other ideas for poses?"

"Maybe one standing without any props?" Michael shrugged.

"We can definitely do that." Emily crossed over to her various background screens and began to pull them down for his approval. She went through every color until she came to the black one. He pointed to it. "That."

"Step up here."

Michael waltzed over to the black backdrop and stood in front with his hands dug deep into his pockets.

"Do you mind?" Emily reached for his full head of hair.

He shook his head.

She ran her hands through his slick-backed hair and messed it up some. "That's better." A smile crossed her lips.

When she was finished with Michael, it was Moon's turn. Who names their daughter Moon? She drew in a deep breath as she decided how to best make Moon look like a runway material.

"Have you ever worn your hair up?" Emily asked.

The girl shook her head.

Emily walked over to her drawers of props and produced a huge tortoise shell hair clip. She also grabbed some powder. This poor girl's face was blotchy, and if she wanted the pictures to come out good, something had to be done.

"Here, let's see what your hair would look like." She handed Moon the clip.

She stared at it as if it were a foreign piece of material

she'd never laid eyes on before. Being a bit impatient, Emily took it out of her hand and began to twist her long but thin hair behind her head, securing it with the clip. She moved from the back and looked at her. She reached up and pulled down a few wisps to hang across her forehead and started powdering her face.

"Wait." Moon pushed Emily's hand away. "What is that?"

"It's theatrical powder. Don't worry, these are individual compacts, and I never use the same one on someone. I'll give it to you to take." She moved her hand toward her face again.

She pulled back, staying out of Emily's reach. "Is it natural? I only wear natural products."

"I don't know, Moon, but if you want to be a model, the makeup artists are going to use a bunch of unnatural stuff on your face. You can't have a blotchy complexion and dark circles under your eyes in your portfolio. You'll never get a call-back." Emily folded her arms.

"Let her fix you up, babe," Michael said in his most coaxing voice.

Emily turned her head and studied him, still wondering what he saw in her. "Shall I continue?" She held out the sponge with the powder caked on it, ready to cover all of Moon's imperfections so they could resume the shoot.

"Okay, but I have to say, I don't approve. I mean, what if they used animals in making this stuff?"

Emily laughed. "I only buy products that have the seal on them that say no animal products were used. We're good!" She buffed on the powder and asked if she could add some blush and maybe some lip gloss. Moon reluctantly agreed. When she was all dolled up, and Emily peered at her through the lens; she couldn't believe the transformation. Maybe this kid would make it in Hollywood after all.

For the couples' portion, she took a few of them holding hands and gazing into each other's eyes and another with him wrapping his arms around her waist, his chin resting on her shoulder as they both looked off into the distance. In Emily's mind, that was the best one by far.

She told them she'd have their prints ready in a few days. She was beginning to get a bit backlogged but promised to get them out as soon as possible. "It was nice meeting you both. I'll be in touch."

After they exited the studio, Emily fetched Daisy. Daisy, like some dog inflicted with rabies, shot through the studio barking, sniffing, and running to every spot the couple had stood.

"What has gotten into you, Daisy?" Emily raised her voice.

But Daisy didn't listen. She was too out of control. Finally, Emily picked her up. "Stop it. Bad girl. I can't wait for our appointment with Dr. Johnson."

EMILY SHOOK the woman's hand. "I've heard great things about you, Dr. Johnson."

Dr. Johnson patted the examining table. "Let's have a look at Daisy."

Emily lifted her onto the chrome table and rubbed her neck while Dr. Johnson did the examination. "Good strong heart," she said, listening with the stethoscope. She prodded and poked her belly, and finished by doing the old temperature in the backside. Emily raised her brows in anticipation of Daisy reacting, but she didn't flinch.

"She's healthy. I'll run some blood work to be sure there is no underlying medical issue, but seems it's more behavioral at this point."

"Yes, she was traumatized when we were held at gunpoint. Ever since that day, she doesn't like men especially, but overall, her behavior has gotten out of control."

Crossing her arms, Dr. Johnson sat back into her chair. "I'd like to start her on some calming medication. Let's see how that goes. Also, do you have any guy friends who could come over and socialize with her, you know, to gain her trust again in men?"

Emily thought about it. She didn't have any male friends. She had some acquaintances, but her best bud was Kayla. A fleeting image of Kayla's brother popped in her brain. "There might be," she said under her breath.

"That's my suggestion at this point." She handed Emily a box of medication. "One every eight hours. Call me in a few days and let me know how she's doing. I'll have the blood results back by then as well." She walked Emily to the waiting room.

"Thank you, Dr. Johnson. I appreciate your help. Daisy is everything to me." Her eyes began to mist.

Dr. Johnson patted her shoulder. "Don't worry. We'll figure it all out. If this doesn't work, I have another ace up my sleeve." A warm smile sparked a smile in return from Emily.

CHAPTER 5

*E*mily agreed to meet Kayla and Connor at the restaurant at six. Her thumping heart told her she was more than a tad excited about seeing him again. She had to play it cool. A guy like Connor, who had women swooning over him constantly wouldn't want her gushing over him like some overbearing groupie. No, she had to do better than that. She'd be mature, sophisticated, cool yet charming.

She glanced around once inside the restaurant, letting her eyes adjust to the dimly lit space. They decided to meet at a well-known Asian place the stars visited regularly. Connor had to maintain his prominence in the acting community.

She got a glimpse of Kayla's head. She could see his profile if she squinted. She made her way to the back of the restaurant where they were both sitting on oversized cushions on the floor with a black lacquer table with mother-of-pearl maidens scenery painted on it. She giggled as she approached them.

"Hey, Emily," Kayla said, jumping up.

They hugged.

"You remember my brother Connor?"

Connor stood and extended his hand.

Emily could feel her face turn red. "Of course. Hi, Connor," she squeaked out.

Kayla plopped back down on the cushion. Emily sat next to her.

"We haven't ordered food yet," Kayla said, picking up her cup and daintily taking a sip of the hot brew.

They talked among themselves about what to order. When the server came, they were ready. They ordered Mongolian beef, lemon chicken, and fried rice. They each ordered a cocktail made with sake. The conversation at first was limited to Kayla and Connor mostly catching up. Then he turned his attention on her.

"So, Kayla tells me you have a photo studio."

"Yes," she said, finishing her gulp of tea. "I just opened it. It's been great. No more traveling for photo shoots. Well, at least it has cut down a lot. There are still some clients who want certain places as their backdrop. I try to accommodate everyone the best I can." She looked down at the table and studied the intricate detail of the mother-of-pearl art.

"That's fantastic. I also heard about your episode with the crazy people."

No matter how hard she tried, that story always came back front and center. She nodded.

"What happened exactly?" he asked.

"I don't like to talk about it much. It's put a damper on how I look at things. And poor Daisy. She hates men now."

Connor shot a strange look over to Kayla, then gazed back at Emily.

"Daisy?"

"My dog. She's a corgi. I've had her for a long time. I can attest to her sweet nature. She loves everyone, from kids to old men and women. She'd lick you to death, not a mean bone in her tiny blue merle body."

Kayla interrupted Emily. "See, Daisy attacked the man and tried to chew him a new one while waiting for the cops."

Connor nodded. "So now she sees all guys as bad. That's a shame."

"I've taken her to a dog behaviorist. We're trying a few things. But until she reverts back to my sweet Daisy, I have to keep her away and locked up from people. She tries to bite them."

Emily didn't dare mention the man friend idea the doctor suggested. It was too early in the evening. So instead she ordered a second sake cocktail and ate entirely too much food.

After dinner, it got awkward. The threesome stood out in the parking lot, making small talk. When the conversation repeated itself, Emily took the opportunity to tell Kayla and Connor good night.

"Hey, Emily," Connor called out as his body slipped into the front passenger seat. "Maybe we can grab a cup of coffee sometime." Then he shut the door.

"Sure, that would be great," she said, quietly knowing full well he didn't hear her reply.

~

SHE INSERTED the key to her apartment and entered the room. Since the incident, she began to leave lights on whenever she went away. Maybe *she* needed some of those calming pills. Daisy stretched out of her sleeping position, a donut, and yawned. Then she padded into the kitchen looking for a treat, wiggling her back end and sending a smile to Emily's face. She sighed. It wasn't her fault she became Cujo. She tossed her a biscuit then headed off to bed with a full tummy and a bit light-headed from the drinks.

CHAPTER 6

The calming pills seemed to be working on Daisy. Emily took her out to the park, and as they made their way toward a group of children jumping rope, Emily held her breath. Daisy trotted by, and when one of the children called out, "Hey lady, you have a cute dog," Emily gave her a backhanded waved and told her thanks. "Can I pet her," the little girls said, running up to them. Emily gasped. But it was too late. The little redheaded girl, with dangling pigtails that curled up on the ends and a freckled face, reached over and petted Daisy. Daisy turned and licked the little girl's hand. Then a boy ran up. This would be the test. "Can I pet her?" He dropped to his knees, now almost on Daisy's level and began scratching her neck. What was it with these kids? They didn't even wait for the green light to pet her. "Aww, she's a sweet dog," the little girl said.

A mother of one of the children called the kids back. Emily waved to her while gently nudging Daisy by pulling on the leash. They finished their walk without incident. Emily held her head high. Things were looking up.

EMILY LISTENED as the person on the other end of the phone pitched her request. She'd been involved with charity work before. Once you gave time and your money, they had your name, and they never let loose of you. She chuckled as the young woman pleaded for her help. It actually was right up her alley. A charity event with stars and their pets, giving all proceeds to a local shelter. A band, food, mingling, and photos. It sounded perfect. "Okay, I'm in," she found herself saying.

There was a small catch. They wanted her to be the organizer and the photographer!

After it all settled into her brain what she volunteered to do, she got a bit nervous. Could she pull it off? It would mean hiring a band, finding someone to cater the event, get some sponsors to help pay for it all, and sitting back and watching the money roll in. Yeah, something like that. She dropped her head back against the sofa cushion. *I'll need some help. Who can help me?* Her gaze rested on Daisy softly snoring on the rug near her feet, and she remembered her dinner with Kayla and Connor. She picked up her phone and stared at it before hitting her number.

She couldn't believe how easy that went. Kayla didn't even bat an eyelash on the details. She said she'd ask around about a caterer and see if Connor had any connections with a band. They agreed on a date to have the event, and like a wildfire, planning went out of control.

In between planning the charity event, Emily had taken Connor up on his invitation for coffee. As she sat across from him, she held her cup with a death grip, waiting for the conversation to flow like it did during dinner two weeks ago. Only now they didn't have Kayla to keep things moving. It was just them. She cleared her throat. "So, is it everything you always dreamed it would be?" She drew the cup to her lips and tested it, then took a bigger taste.

"Yes, and more. But it's like super crazy, too. It's so different than stage performance. With all the takes, we only do small segments at a time. It's exhausting."

"That's what I've heard," she said.

"I found a nice apartment walking distance to the studio, though. I thought New York was expensive." He laughed, and his eyes danced in rhythm.

She swallowed down the lump before she continued. Something about him made her hands sweat and her pulse race.

"Did Kayla mention to you about the charity event I'm planning?"

"No. Is there anything I can do to help?" He reached across the table, resting his hand on hers.

Daisy let out a low rumble from under the table where she'd been observing.

"Daisy," Emily said firmly.

"I see she's still a bit aggressive," he said, looking under the table.

"Not aggressive. She's been through a lot," Emily said with a tone of defensiveness that even surprised her. "We're working through some things," she said in a softer, kinder tone.

"I know. What you two went through was horrible." He let Daisy sniff his hand.

Emily held her breath.

Daisy sniffed, nudging him gently with her nose.

"She's warming up to me," he said.

"Would you like to come over one night?" she blurted.

He pulled his head up from under the table and studied her.

"I mean so that you can get used to Daisy."

"Why would I have to get used to her?" His deep stare took her breath away.

Her mouth dry as the Sahara Desert made her tongue stick to the roof of her mouth. She stretched for the cup and drew in a sip. "This is awkward," she said.

He laid his hand on hers. "It doesn't have to be." His sexy bravado made her shiver.

"I don't expect us to pick up where we left off, but—"

"I was hoping we would," he said, cutting her off.

"Why don't you come over tonight. We can discuss this charity event I agreed to do that I'm quite sure I'm in over my head on." She flashed him a warm smile.

"Together we'll tackle it. Two heads are better than one."

She tapped her finger to her cheek as she considered his offer. "Well, now that you mention it, yes, I believe you can help. I need to find a caterer and a band, and also some sponsors. Maybe some of your acting friends would like to help?"

"I could ask the actors guild if they'd like to sponsor it. What's the charity?"

"We're raising funds for the shelters here in the county. So many animals are awaiting their forever home.

It makes me sad to think about all of them sitting in cages while they wait."

"I know you love animals. Let me see what I can do to help. Where is the event going to be held at, and when?"

Emily dropped her hands to the table. "Kayla and I picked a date, but I totally forgot about the venue!"

"Okay, don't panic. We can figure this out. Let me make a few calls. I'm new in town, but I've made a few friends. Do you know how many people are expected to come to something like this?"

"Yeah, about that…"

Connor furrowed his brows. "That many, huh?"

She nodded.

SHE OPENED a box of crackers and piled some onto a plate. She sliced cheese and summer sausage and arranged them around the outside. Twisting the cap off the brand-new jar of olives, she dipped the spoon inside, retrieving several. She brought down two stemless glasses from the cabinet, popped the cork of a good bottle of red wine and started her playlist, making sure the volume was low, and waited.

A light tap on her door sent Daisy into a barking fit.

"Daisy!"

Daisy stopped.

"Good girl," Emily said with one hand on the doorknob.

She let Connor inside, and the two stood in the entryway while Daisy checked him out, sniffing both shoes and part of his pant leg. Satisfied he wasn't an intruder, she let him take a few steps into the living area.

"I'm sorry."

"No worries." Connor chuckled.

"Please, have a seat. I made us a snack."

Emily fetched the platter filled with goodies and brought it to the coffee table. Connor's eyes lit up. "I'll have red."

She drew her head back and laughed. "How'd you know I was going to offer you a glass of wine?"

He pointed to the meat and cheese platter.

She nodded left to right as she pursed her lips. "I guess it gave it away. Well, it so happens I opened a red. That's my choice, and I was hoping it would be yours as well." She walked into the kitchen.

"Listen, I spoke to a few people about the charity event. I think I got some stuff started."

"Oh, that's great," she said, raising her voice a bit as she poured the wine.

She handed him a glass and took a seat in a chair opposite him.

"I don't bite," he said with that same low, sexy voice.

She gulped quietly. "I know," she said teasingly.

He reached for the plate, grabbing a slice of cheese, tossing it into his mouth and devouring it in one bite. Then he went for the sausage.

"So, tell me more about the help you've enlisted." She drew the glass to her mouth and took a sip.

"Got a lead on a band that might be available, and the name of a restaurant that might provide the catering. I have a few more details to get, but I should have something more concrete to tell you by Thursday. I didn't realize how quickly bands and caterers book up."

She crossed her legs and sat back deep into the chair, munching on a cracker. "I didn't either. You'd think with a place as big as L.A., there would be tons of bands and choices."

"I thought that too." He smiled.

"Looks like Daisy has given you the seal of approval." Emily motioned over to Daisy with her head.

Connor looked down. At his feet sat Daisy, peering up.

"She's waiting for a treat," Emily said.

He broke a small piece of cheese off and fed it to her. Daisy chowed it down.

"Did she even taste it?" Connor laughed.

"Probably not."

Daisy wagged her tail and barked.

"Okay, one more piece," Emily said in a playful scolding.

Connor obliged the begging corgi by giving her another small bite.

"She's definitely a chow hound," he said.

"Oh, for sure. That's why we have to walk so much. Keep the unwanted pounds away."

"You surely don't have to lose any. You're perfect the way you are." His eyes gleamed.

She raised her hand to her cheeks. "Now you're going to embarrass me."

"No, I mean it. You are beautiful the way you are."

"I used to be much thinner, but lately, I've been eating more than I should. Stress eating."

"Because of the incident?" He cocked his head as he listened.

"Yeah. It really did affect me as well. For nights, I had bad dreams of people busting in and waving guns around."

"Have you thought about taking a self-defense class?"

Emily giggled. "I'm trained. I know a few moves that would bring you down to your knees."

He held out his hands. "Whoa, no thanks. I like everything the way it is."

"It still affected me. He had a gun. You have to be quick with martial arts when someone pulls a gun on you," she said, reaching for a slice of cheese and an olive.

"How about learning to shoot? I thought about it too," he said.

"Want to go together?" She raised her brows.

"Yes. Whenever you're ready."

"Let's get this event off the ground first. We're making progress with Daisy, so that's good. We'll get the charity going. We can think about us later."

"Us?"

"I...I..." she stuttered.

"I'm teasing. I understand. Shooting. It's all about the gun range." He winked.

CHAPTER 7

She'd been on the phone all morning. Breathing heavy, she leashed up Daisy, grabbed her keys, and with the phone held between her shoulders and ear, rushed out to her car.

"Yes, I understand. You couldn't possibly help us at this late date. Thanks for calling me back."

She opened the car door and lifted Daisy into the seat. She drove over to the studio and waited for her first client of the day. As a test of Daisy's continued progress, she let her roam around the open space. If it were true that dogs could sense nervousness or anxiety, Daisy should be on full alert about now. With her heart beating a mile a minute, Emily waited for them to arrive. An older actress who was quite the interest back in the day was coming with her daughter and granddaughter for a generational picture. But if the past was any indication, her driver, Earl, would also be coming.

Emily quickly welcomed the group inside and immediately smiled. She loved doing this kind of shoot. Each of them wore an outfit with blue and white. The grandmother had on a blue chiffon blouse and wide leg slacks in white, with white sandals. Her daughter had on a blue-and-white print sleeveless dress, and her granddaughter had on a solid blue capped-sleeve dress with white strappy block heel sandals.

Earl shuffled in. If Emily guessed his age, he was probably close to Claire's age. In fact, somewhere in the back of her mind, she remembered hearing a rumor about them. He took a seat. Daisy waltzed over to him, sniffed him once, then turned away. Happy she didn't growl or bite him, Emily went to work.

"Everyone is so coordinated!" Emily said as she began placing them in their positions.

She stood back, tapping her finger to her mouth. She stepped toward the grandmother and moved her from the first spot to the middle. She bobbed back a few steps and admired the smiling faces. "Yes, that looks good."

After they did a few poses, the threesome took off with their driver. Emily had about twenty minutes before the next client's appointment. This time, a baby. She loved doing those, too, and she was told they were bringing the family pet.

She devoured a granola bar and a bottled water. She popped a few grapes into her mouth and had just finished washing them down when they arrived. Only a few days old, the precious bundle of joy with rosy cheeks made Emily want to kiss her tiny little body from her ten fingers to her ten toes. She resisted the urge. Rufus the family pet, a black and white spaniel, sat quietly waiting his turn.

Mom quickly disrobed baby Charlotte and secured a

headband around her little hairless head that sported a pink flower. Emily motioned to the black velvet blanket she'd draped across a chair.

"I think she'll look so cute here."

Mom gently placed her on her belly. Emily went to work placing her head resting on her hands and propping up her bottom slightly for the pose. Then she rushed to her camera and began to click away. She'd already been told she had an hour before feeding time. Rufus got in a few of the pictures as well.

Satisfied the pictures would come out darling, Emily assured the happy couple she'd forward the prints soon.

She picked up her phone. She had a missed call from Connor. She sat down to catch her breath before her next and final client of the day arrived and returned his call.

"Hey," he said. "How's your day going?"

"Good. I'm in between clients. I photographed the cutest six-day-old baby. I wanted to eat her toes she was so precious." Emily giggled.

"Eat her toes, huh? Glad you didn't share that with the new parents. They might have called the men in blue on ya." He laughed.

"Whatever. She was so darling. Anyway, what's up?"

"I think I got a few more leads on some donors. A friend of mine from back in New York said he's good for a large donation. He said he'll drop by the event and present it to you."

"Oh, anyone I know?" she said teasingly.

"Chris Ryan."

"Chris Ryan! *The* Chris Ryan? The swoon-worthy, every girl's dream, Chris Ryan?"

"Okay, I get it. You think he's handsome. Yes, that Chris Ryan. You can stop drooling."

She reached over and grabbed a paper napkin sitting on the table and wiped the drool. How'd he know? "I'm not drooling, but he is super cute. Good job, Connor!"

"Anyway, back to the event…"

"I'm sorry. I'm really teasing. It's hard to see over the phone lines. It's like texting. Never comes off the way I mean it. He's good-looking, but he's not my type. Do you feel better now?" She softened her voice to try to calm the situation.

"Much."

"I wanted to ask you out to dinner," he said, boldly taking the conversation to a different place.

"That's not necessary. You can come over here, and I can make us a snack. We can brainstorm over a glass of wine," she said.

"I'm asking you out on a date, Emily."

The silence so thick you could slice it with a knife penetrated the airways.

"Hello?" he said.

"I'm here. I'm trying to register what you said."

"I think I'm getting mixed signals here. I thought you liked me?"

"I do. I like you very much." She let out a slow breath.

"So, what's the problem? Don't you date?"

"Of course, I date. I dated you once, remember?" Her voice held a sliver of resentment.

"Yes, so I was hoping we could maybe pick up where we left off."

"You said that already," she bantered back, enjoying the back and forth tempo they had going.

"Come on, Emily. I know you like me."

She knew his blue eyes were twinkling and he was probably batting those long lashes she loved. She let out a long sigh. "Okay, it's a date. Where are you going to take me?" She continued teasing for a bit longer.

"La Joliesse. They have a wonderful chef. You'll love it."

"Lyra St. Claire is the chef, right?"

"Yes, have you dined there before?"

"No. I've wanted to, but it's not the sort of place one goes to by themselves. Besides, I hear it's a long wait to get in."

"Yeah, normally a long wait, but she and I go way back."

"Were you on her show?" Emily asked.

"A long time ago."

"I met her before," Emily said nonchalantly.

"Oh? And when were you going to let on with this tidbit of news?"

"After you stopped bragging."

"Me, brag?" he snickered.

"I met her at a wedding. I got called in to do the photography for Eden Love and Aaron Carter because their first choice couldn't fit it in their schedule. Then because Lyra liked my work so much, she called me to shoot the spread for a magazine she'd be in. That's how I became a bit enamored with corgis, too. She had little Cinnamon, and well, I got hooked."

"Maybe she'll be there when we have our date. I can't wait to see you."

His low, gravelly voice drew her right in. She closed her eyes and let the warm waves of his tone drift through her, sending shivers down her spine and the hair on her arms to stand. She brushed her arms with her hands and replied, "I can't wait to see you, either."

CHAPTER 8

$\mathcal{E}$mily tried to keep her head out of the clouds while she stayed vigilant on finding donors for the event. She knocked on a lot of doors only to find a few slammed in her face. She sat in her car, pondering her tactics in asking for not only their time but their money. She laid her head back onto the seat rest. "Rich people can be so stingy sometimes," she said out loud.

She pulled up quickly. "Ah-ha! I think I have it." She ran her hands through her long dark hair. Gathering it into a bundle, she then let her thick strands slip out of her clasp. She started her engine and sped off.

La Joliesse, the restaurant Connor was taking her to, was trendy yet casual with an upscale feeling. Upscale and casual were complete opposites in her mind. Did she wear jeans or a dress? Scratching her head, she looked into her closet. A burnt orange sundress caught her eye. With her long dark hair and olive complexion, this shade seemed to be her friend. She received many compliments when she wore that dress. It was casual but nice. She searched the many pairs of shoes she owned and drew out a strappy brown sandal with a chunky heel. This was about as much upscale as she could get. She didn't own a single fancy gown, or glittery outfit unless you counted her Christmas sweater she wore every year. Her go-to "fancy" wear was a pair of black chiffon wide leg pants and a frilly white blouse she paired it with. One of these days she'd have to break down and buy a gown.

After she dressed and fixed her hair, she applied a light foundation, darkened her lashes with black mascara, dusted some brown eye shadow on her lids and applied some pink gloss to her lips. She stood back and studied herself in the mirror. Scrunching up her face with her gaze darting from her hair to her face and down her body, she squarely landed her fix on her ears. Earrings. I need hoops. She rummaged through her unorganized jewelry box, looking for earrings. She grabbed the hoops she thought would look good and went back to the mirror. Stepping back after she put on the jewelry, a coy smile slipped across her mouth. Now she was complete.

"OH WOW. YOU LOOK FANTASTIC," he said, making her blush.

"Thank you."

"Are you ready?"

"Yes, but come in and say hi to Daisy."

Connor stepped inside and immediately encountered

the almost completely normal Daisy. "How's my girl doing?" He scratched her head, then behind her ears, baby-talking to her the entire time.

Daisy licked him.

"She seems to be herself again, huh?" His bedroom eyes made her squirm.

She nodded.

"So glad. I know you were really worried about her."

Emily gripped her brown crossover purse and giving Daisy a pat on the head, ushered Connor out, closing the door behind them.

She watched as he moved toward the parked car. Showing off his physique, the dark somewhat tight-fitting, straight-leg jeans paired with the free-flowing linen shirt in a soft shade of blue—with the first three buttons undone—made her mouth water. Now she knew what upscale meant for sure in L.A. It meant whatever floated your boat. This Texas girl was catching on fast!

He opened the door for her, and she slid onto soft leather seats. She got a whiff of the leather as she placed the seat belt over her. When he slid in next to her, she got a whiff of him. Spicy, earthy…so darn desirable.

"Hope you're hungry." He turned toward her and smiled.

If only he knew. "Yes, I'm starving."

He put the car in gear, and tearing off down the street, showed off a bit before he slowed down. "I love to see her go fast for a bit." He chuckled.

"It's a powerful car," she said, enjoying the thrill of the speed.

"Any more luck with securing donors for the event?"

"A couple. But you know what I realized after about

the third rejection?" She wobbled slightly to look at him. She couldn't get enough of him. His profile was as handsome.

"No, what?"

"Rich people are cheap."

He cut her a strange look, then put his eyes back on the road.

"Seriously. If you ask them for money, they like clam up. What's that about? I give money all the time to charities."

"I don't think you can fairly put all rich people into the same basket," he said.

"Maybe not, but it's been my experience." Shrugging, she sat back into her seat and stared out the windshield.

When they arrived at the restaurant, they were greeted by a friendly face who promptly seated them. Soon their server appeared, ready to tell them about the specials and take their drink order.

Emily casually looked around at the tables. Her gaze drifted, hoping to land on someone famous. But by the dripping diamonds the women wore, and the Rolex watches on the men's wrists, everything about that restaurant and its patrons said rich and famous.

"I'm so happy we got in tonight." He peered over the menu.

"I hope you didn't have to promise to name your first-born after her or anything like that," she said.

"Nothing quite that serious."

"But you did have to do some sort of favor, right?" She kept on him with the questions.

"Not exactly. Like I said, Lyra and I go way back. We have a connection." He lowered his eyes to the menu.

"Filet mignon." He closed the menu and tossed it on the table.

She picked up her menu and glanced the entrees. "Ooh. I see what I want already." She closed her menu and sat it beside her plate. "Salmon is one of my all-time favorites. If a chef knows what they are doing, it will be prepared perfectly."

At first, it was total silence as they dined. Emily's salmon was prepared to perfection, and she savored each and every bite. Shaking her head, she sat back. "Yep. She knows what she's doing."

"My filet melted in my mouth like butter," he said, nodding.

"My salmon too."

When the server came to the table to ask how they were enjoying the meal, Emily expressed her desire. "So delicious."

"If you could tell the chef that Connor Stone is dining here this evening, I would appreciate that." He winked at the young woman.

"I thought that was you." She blushed as she spoke, making Emily giggle. "I'll let Lyra know you are here." She rushed away from the table, leaving the two alone once again.

Emily leaned forward. "Did you see her blush? You made her day, Connor!"

"Quit it," he said, slapping at her hand.

A beautiful woman with long, red wavy hair, brilliant green eyes, and full lips stood before them. Connor jumped up and hugged her. Emily focused on the pair.

"It's so good to see you, Connor." She quickly pecked him on the cheek.

"This is my friend, Emily King. She's a photographer."

"Emily! It's so nice to see you again." She pulled her in and kissed her on one cheek, then the other. Stepping back with her hands resting on Emily's shoulders, her gaze drifted over to Connor. "I had no idea you two were a thing." She released her hold on Emily and stepped back.

"She and my sister are best friends."

"Ah, I see. Well, what did you think of your dinner?"

"The salmon was cooked to perfection."

"I'm so happy you enjoyed it. We use the sous vide cooking method here," she said, crossing her arms.

"Was my steak prepared that way as well?" Connor asked.

She nodded. "Yes, we prepare almost all our protein that way. It makes the meat more tender."

"Thanks for making a spot for us tonight." He gazed at the bustling crowd.

"I try to help out friends when I can. The trouble is, everyone in this industry wants to be your friend."

"Lyra," Emily said, interrupting. "I'm organizing a charity event. It's to help the homeless animals here in the L.A. area. Perhaps you could do something for the event. I'm searching for donors."

"I'd love to help out. Count me in for a large donation."

"I think that would be awesome. I'm trying to find someone to cater the event. You wouldn't know anyone, would you?

"I wish I could help you, but we're slammed here. I do have a wonderful baker on staff as well. She's actually a chef in training. Maybe she'll have an idea. I must get back to the kitchen. It was nice seeing you again." She turned to Connor, holding out her hands. He clasped his with hers.

"It was great to see you again. You're as handsome as ever. Enjoy your visit to L.A."

"I'm not visiting here. I live here now."

She dropped her hands from his. "Get out!"

"No, seriously. I'm making a movie. Should be out in time for the December runs."

"Oh, that's great news, Connor. Then I shall see you again soon, huh?" She winked then blew past them both on her way back to the kitchen.

Emily rocked back on her heels. "Wow. She's great. Talk about outgoing. Every time I see her, I'm amazed at her energy."

"I don't think she realizes how much appeal she has," Connor said, staring off toward the direction she headed.

Emily knitted her brows.

He pulled her in toward him, a disappointing guise spread across his face. "Not like that, Emily."

"How'd you know what I was thinking?"

"I could see the wheels turning." He dropped a kiss on her forehead.

Their first kiss. At La Joliesse.

"I'm not the jealous type. Really." She lowered her head.

He pulled his arms out from her waist and dangled one arm over her shoulder. He tossed a couple of hundred-dollar bills onto the table as he led her out of the restaurant.

CHAPTER 9

"Hey, it's me. Your best friend who hasn't really been much of a friend lately. Call me." Emily tossed the phone onto the counter. She lowered her gaze to Daisy. "I don't blame her if she doesn't call right back. I've been a terrible friend lately."

The phone rang and vibrated, dancing across the counter. Emily's eyes flew open. "I knew she cared." She quickly answered it. "Hi, Kayla."

"Hi." Her response was short and not all that sweet.

"I'm sorry I haven't been around for you lately. Daisy had to see a shrink, and I've been super busy with shoots. It's such a busy time of the year for me."

"Don't forget dating," she said with a hint of smugness that raised Emily's brows.

"You heard about that, did you?"

"Remember, he is my brother," she said, elevating her voice.

Emily walked around the counter with the phone

glued to her ear. "Yes, I know. Listen, have lunch with me today."

"Where?"

"Meet me at Joe's around noon."

"Okay. I'll be the girl with the sad eyes because I haven't seen my friend in a few weeks."

Kayla's play-cry made her laugh. "Yeah, right. So sad. Nothing like nachos piled high with grilled chicken, guacamole, and salsa to perk you right up. See you at noon."

Joe's was a little hole-in-wall café that made the best nachos. A few outdoor tables with umbrellas was the perfect spot to enjoy the food, sunny weather, and people watch. Emily's light calendar for the day allowed her to make room for Kayla; she had a lot of making up to do. It always seemed to work this way. When one of them got a boyfriend, the other one got left out.

SHE KISSED Kayla on the cheek before sitting. She nodded toward the lime-colored drink. "You started without me."

Emily held up her hand to get the attention of the server.

"I ordered the nachos too. They should be out any minute."

Emily knitted her brows.

"You said noon. I expected you to be on time."

Emily laughed. "I'm only five minutes late. The traffic was horrific."

"L.A." Kayla sipped her drink.

"So, how have you been?" Emily tilted her head.

"Good. I'm seeing someone."

Emily straightened her back. "Oh?"

"His name is Spencer. He's a double."

"Double for whom?"

"Parker Collins."

Emily arched her brows to her hairline. "He's a hottie."

"Who, Parker or Spencer?" Kayla asked.

Emily began to speak, but Kayla waved her off. "Oh yeah, right. I get it. If Parker is a hottie, Spencer must be too." She laughed off her ditzy moment.

"Anyway…tell me about him," Emily persisted.

"He's a little shy, but I sort of like that. He's cute, but we've already established that. He's kind, and he loves animals."

"Does he love his momma too?" Emily winked.

"Yes, for the record."

The server sat the huge platter of nachos in the middle. "Can I get you anything else?"

The girls tossed glances back and forth, replying "no thank you" in unison.

"I'm so happy you have a new friend," Emily said in between bites.

"Me, too, 'cuz my other friend deserted me."

"She did not. She's been super busy. Why don't you come over this weekend? Bring Spencer. I'm sure Connor would love to meet him. We can order pizza, play charades, and get to know him."

They finished their lunch, getting caught up, and before they said goodbye, Kayla asked about Daisy.

"You said something about her having to see a shrink."

"She was having some issues regarding the whole gun episode. She's doing much better."

"What was she doing?"

"Hating on men." Emily tsked.

"Well, she'll love Spencer."

EMILY WRAPPED up her last shoot. Kayla was coming over and bringing Spencer. Game night should be laid-back. The food and drink should be equally relaxed. She and Daisy headed to the store where she picked up a vegetable platter, some boneless chicken wings, and a big bag of chips. As she pushed the shopping cart up to the register, she did an inventory of her basket.

Daisy let out a whisper of a growl. Emily shook her finger at her. "Bad girl. No growling." Looking around, she made eye contact with some dude waiting in line behind her. She gave him a quick half smile as she put her groceries on the conveyor. Daisy growled again.

This time Emily apologized. "I'm really sorry about her growling. She's going through this thing."

"No worries," the guy said.

Emily paid for her items and left the store carrying her bags and pulling Daisy along on the leash. "I don't under-stand you," she said as she put her in the seat, then tossed her bags in the back. She hurried to the other side when she ran smack into the guy from the store.

She jumped back. "Oh, hey," she said, stumbling back into the car.

The man now had a smirk, and because of his proximity to her, she could also smell booze on him.

"Listen, I don't want any trouble. Let me get in my car and go."

"I saw the way you smiled at me in the store. You want some of this," he said, pumping his hand on his chest.

Just then a little déjà vu crept in. "No. No, I don't. I want to get in my car and go." She tried to keep her panicked tone to a minimum.

"Ah, come on pretty little lady. Let's party!" He grabbed at her hands.

Emily kicked him in the leg, snatched him around the neck, and threw him down on the ground. And for good measure, she stood on his hand. "Don't ever underestimate a woman again. You may not live to talk about it." She straightened her torso, flipped her hair back, and jumped into her car.

Shaken but not totally distracted, she made her way back to her apartment. "Daisy, you were a good girl after all. You knew that guy was up to no good. I need to learn to trust your intuitions." She patted her on the head. "I love you, girl. You've saved me twice from bad guys."

EMILY FRESHENED up after her little fiasco at the grocery store parking lot. While the boneless chicken wings were heating up in the oven, she tidied up the apartment and sprayed Daisy with some dog fragrance she got at the pet store.

Kayla arrived with Spencer in tow, followed by Connor. After the introductions and Connor sizing up Spencer for a few minutes, the group settled in with drinks and food and soon a game of charades. While the three were guessing what in the world Kayla was describing for them to guess, Emily told them what had happened to her earlier at the grocery store.

"What?" Connor said, his voice loud and strong.

"I took care of it. I have skills," Emily said, showing a martial arts move with her hands.

"Okay, but what if he had—"

"A gun?" Kayla said, finishing his sentence for him.

Connor nodded. "Yes, a gun."

"I would have taken it away from him like I did the last time someone tried that." Emily picked up a wing and gnawed on it.

"You have a little something," Connor said, motioning to her chin.

She quickly wiped it away with a nearby napkin. She continued eating.

"I have all these feelings right now," Kayla said.

Connor leaned over and whispered in Emily's ear. "Wine sadness."

Emily cocked her head and arched her brows. "Wine sadness?"

"You know. When a girl drinks wine and gets all goopy."

"Goopy? You mean emotional? Caring?" Emily's words were terse. She couldn't help herself.

"Yeah, sappy," Connor said, knocking shoulders with Emily.

"Connor Stone. I swear, you're nothing but a big tease, and during a time such as this."

Spencer cleared his throat. "I know I'm just the guy dating your sister, but I think it's kind of nice she cares about her best friend." The two guys locked stares.

Kayla and Emily's heads bobbed back and forth between the two guys. Finally, Emily spoke.

"I'm deeply touched about Kayla's concern for my welfare. And Connor is too. Aren't you, Connor?" She tapped his leg.

"Yeah, deeply."

"Who needs more chicken." Emily jumped up and made her way to the kitchen.

"I need more wine," Kayla called out right behind her.

While the two women heated up more wings, Kayla dumped more chips into the big blue bowl. "I hate it when two guys have to see who has the most testosterone. I mean really." She chomped on some chips as she watched the two men square off.

"I know. It's like they have to defend us or something. Didn't they hear I beat the stuffing out of a guy?" Emily laughed.

Emily tossed some wings on the platter, Kayla grabbed the bowl of chips, and the two headed back into the ring of fire.

"Okay, you guys. Peace. No more standing off. We get it. You love us. You want us to be safe. End of story. Now let's get back to charades." Emily motioned to Kayla with her chin.

Kayla began to describe her clue.

By the end of the evening, two empty wine bottles sat on the coffee table, a platter empty except for remnants of sauce, a few crumbled chips in the bottom of the bowl, a couple of broccoli pieces, and a few carrot sticks. Slumped in the chair, Connor could hardly keep his eyes open, Kayla was sleeping on the crux of Spencer's shoulder, and Spencer was snoring softly. Emily leashed up

Daisy for a night walk before they would head to bed. She had one hand on the door when Connor spoke.

"I'm coming with you."

They walked Daisy. She sniffed a few bushes before she found her spot.

"What a beautiful night," Emily said, looking at the stars.

Connor slid his arm over her shoulder. "I'm sorry about tonight. I like Spencer. He and Kayla are good together."

Emily nodded. "I think so too."

Daisy tugged the leash; she wanted to walk further. Emily and Connor obliged.

"Emily," he said, stopping and turning her toward him.

"Yes."

"I know we recently started dating, but we've known each other for a while. Do you think it would be all right to kiss you?"

"I thought you'd never ask." She leaned in.

While he held her head, he stroked her cheek, sending goose bumps up and down her arms. He gazed into her eyes. "You're so beautiful," he said.

He lowered his mouth, his lips brushing over hers. She reached up and cupped her hands around his neck and held him while they kissed under the stars.

CHAPTER 10

When they entered the apartment, they found both Kayla and Spencer still asleep. Connor walked over to the sink and filled a cup with water.

"Connor Stone, don't you dare," Emily warned.

He walked up to them quietly, then dipped his hand in the cup to his fingertips. He quickly pulled them out, shaking them in their faces. Both of them drew up from their position, wiping the droplets from their cheeks.

"Time to wake up, you two," he said, stepping back.

Kayla stretched and yawned while Spencer rubbed his eyes, then ran his hand across his chin. They stumbled to the kitchen where they both drank a glass of water before hitting the road. Now Connor and Emily were left alone. They'd already shared their first serious kiss. The awkwardness should have left them.

Connor began cleaning up the remainder of the mess in the kitchen. Emily clearly saw it for what it was. A delay tactic.

"Hey, leave that. It's late. I can do it in the morning." She flashed him a smile.

"I don't mind. My mom always taught me to play well with others and make sure I clean up my mess when it was time to go home." His eyes sparkled when he spoke of his mom.

She crossed over to him and laced her arms around his waist. "Well, your mother taught you well." She rose on the balls of her feet and planted a quick kiss on his lips.

"I have an early rehearsal tomorrow, so if you're sure?" He tipped his head while nodding for reassurance it was all right to leave.

"Yes." She placed her hand on his back as she guided him toward the front door.

Daisy perked up from her sleeping position.

He stopped before exiting. Whirling around, he brought Emily close and stared deep into her eyes. She wondered if he could read her mind. The thought brought the hairs on the back of her neck to crawl.

"I had a great night. We've been seeing a lot of each other. Are you tired of me yet?"

"Never," she said, low and steady.

"Good, because the thought of not seeing you or at the very least hearing from you each and every day will drive me absolutely crazy." He bent down and kissed her.

"If you keep kissing me like that, you can be assured I'll never get tired of you." She winked.

She lifted her hand, wiggling her fingers at him in a dainty wave as she watched him jog down the walkway. He turned slightly, waving back. "Good night," he called.

"Good night."

OVER THE COURSE of the next few days, Emily busted her chops securing all the final donors for the event. She sat in her car, amazed she'd finally secured the music. It wasn't some first-rate band or even a second, but she listened to a few songs on the demo tape they provided, and she liked what she heard. When she told them it was for an animal charity, they busted out in "Who Let the Dogs Out," making her laugh.

"You're hired! By the way, what's your band's name?"

Their puzzled looks suggested they'd not thought about it before. "We were just some guys in the neighborhood who got together in Jay's garage."

Emily tapped her chin. "How about Jay's Garage Band?"

The guys laughed. Jay spoke. "It will do for now."

"Where are we playing?" a young, skinny guy with tats all down his arm asked.

Emily stumbled on her words. Where were they having it at? Her heart dropped to her feet. She gasped. Grabbing Daisy's leash, yanking her and startling her, she yelled to the guys she'd be in touch. She vaguely recalled seeing their strange looks as she booked out of there.

"Daisy! I almost forgot the most important thing. The venue! We had to make a decision by"—she looked down at her cell—"an hour ago," she whispered. She drove like a bat out of you-know-where to get to the number one choice. She hoped it was still available.

"I'm sorry, Ms. King, it's already been reserved by another event." The woman lifted her shoulders in an apology of sorts.

"It's not your fault. It's mine." She tugged at Daisy's leash, and the two exited the glamorous hotel with their heads hanging low. "I don't know what I'm going to do." She started the engine.

She drove over to her number two pick, and it was the same story. "We booked the venue for that same date two hours ago," a young blonde said.

"Thanks," Emily said with a ring of despondency in her voice.

They drove down the back roads toward home. They'd passed the strawberry fields where school children came for field trips, and families came on the weekend for berries and fun. She put on the brakes and made a hard turn into the lot. She parked the car, grabbed Daisy, and headed for someone that had the look of being in charge. After two false attempts, someone directed her to a person who could help. She told the woman her sob story, and before she could even finish, the bright-eyed woman responded with, "If you want to have it here it's no problem. If you are serving alcohol, we need to see the permit, and I'll give you the form to fill out." She turned and walked toward a faded blue shack that was a makeshift office. Emily let Daisy sniff around.

Emily viewed the dusty fields. It wouldn't be so bad once they put up some huge white canopy-style tents. She could visualize where the band would set up, the temporary bar, and the buffet line. A wooden dance floor with small white hanging lights would make the space warm and inviting.

"Here you go." The woman handed the one-page application to her. "Normally we're booked for weddings this time of year. It's your lucky day." She flashed Emily a smile.

"My lucky day? Well, I guess I should look at it that way." She fetched a pen from her purse and began to fill it out right on the spot. She wasn't going to take any chances on it getting away from her.

"I think I've filled everything out." Emily waited while the woman examined it.

"Looks great. So, I need a check in the amount of one thousand dollars with the rest payable after the event."

Emily scanned the application quickly. Was that anywhere on the form? "How much is the balance?"

The woman knitted her brows. "Didn't you read all the fine print?" She giggled, causing Emily to follow suit.

"It's five thousand dollars to rent this here," she said, motioning wide. "One thousand deposit. The other four after the party."

"That's reasonable. Are there bathrooms out here?"

"You have to contact the porta potty people. They'll truck in some real nice ones. Even a hand washing station." The woman appeared proud of this and widened her smile to prove it.

"Hand washing stations too," Emily said.

What did I get myself into? "Okay, great. Thanks for the info. You have my phone number and email. Guess I'll be shoving off. Thanks again for everything."

When Emily reached for Daisy's leash, she saw the corgi had something in her mouth. "What are you eating?" She removed a ball of slimy red stuff and tossed it into the dirt.

"That's an overripe strawberry," the woman said.

Emily dug in her purse for something to wipe her fingers on.

"This has been a trying day. I'm going home, putting my feet up and closing my eyes while I listen to some soothing music."

"I hope the rest of your day is less trying," the woman said.

"Me too."

Emily set the station in her car to easy listening. "Might as well start now with the soothing music," she said out loud, watching Daisy.

No sooner did she get home, pour herself a tall glass of water, slip her shoes off, and drop to the couch, her phone rang. She tossed her head back. "Ugh!" She picked up the phone lying next to her. "Hey," she said.

"Hey. How's your day going so far?" Connor said, his tone smooth like music to her ears.

She tried to sound perky, but the truth was, she was so worn out between organizing the event, keeping up with her shoots and always on edge with Daisy, wondering when or if she'd become Sybil again.

"It's going okay. I'm so tired. I think I need to beef up on the vitamins." She pulled the glass of water to her lips and took a drink.

"Yeah, so everything is done now regarding the event?" Connor's cheerful voice couldn't help but bring a smile to her.

"Yes, except for one thing. We need a name for it before I get the flyers printed and send out the email to all the publicists."

"We can discuss it tonight over dinner?" His cheerfulness kept coming through the phone.

"Oh, Connor. There's nothing more I'd like, but I'm bushed. Can I take a rain check?"

"Sure," he said curtly, the cheerfulness totally gone from his voice.

"You're not angry, are you?"

"Nope." His short response begged to differ.

"Connor, don't be like that. I've had a rough few days. Tomorrow. Come over tomorrow, and I'll fix you dinner, okay?" she practically begged him.

"I'll see if I can. I don't know. I might have something to do."

She paused before replying. "You might have something to do?"

"Uh-huh. Listen, they're calling me back to the set. I'll talk to you later."

Click.

She held the phone out from her ear. "Did I get a brush off from him?" She tossed the phone next to her, pulled her legs up and placed them on the table, crossing them at the ankle. "I think I did." She closed her eyes, squeezing out a small tear that ran down her cheek.

CHAPTER 11

Sitting at the table sipping on her first cup of coffee, Emily looked over her schedule. She had three clients coming starting at ten. Her gaze drifted to the top of the phone where the time was displayed. She had about an hour. She washed down the other half of her blueberry muffin with the remaining coffee, jumped in the shower, and after getting dressed, headed to the studio with Daisy in tow.

Daisy licked her paws a few times, yawned, then stretched, and rested her head on her paws. She had the routine down.

"You're going to be a good girl today, right?" Emily patted her head.

Once inside, she began to get her equipment ready. Her first appointment was a few head and body shots. Nothing special. She'd never worked with him before. He was referred by a friend of a friend. After that, a family portrait setting and finally an engagement announcement photo. Then off to the office store to get flyers printed, a couple of posters, and afterward, she'd be visiting a few well-known publicists in town to get the word out.

She kept tossing around the few names she'd come up with for the event. She felt bad Connor wasn't able to offer his suggestions. She wasn't up to any company last night. She was betting on he'd forgotten all about it and he'd be back to his charismatic self. One could only hope.

The young fellow who came for his session was on the quiet side. She kept digging, hoping he'd open up.

"Lift your chin slightly and to the left," Emily said, trying to get the best picture.

He did as she asked.

"Relax your shoulders a bit. You look stiff," she said.

He did as she asked.

"So, it says here you're an actor. Have you starred in anything I might know of?" She peered over the camera.

"Probably not."

"Tell me a few," she said, prodding.

"A couple of commercials is all. I'm still waiting for my big break."

"So, you can talk!" She chuckled.

"I'm shy."

"Shy is good. But don't be naïve. One thing I've learned in this business is they'll roll right over you if you are."

"Duly noted."

"I'm organizing a charity event. It's to benefit the shelter animals. It will be held over at the Johnson's Strawberry Fields. An outdoor event. I guess you figured that out. But I need a name for it. I'm getting ready to have flyers printed, and I haven't finalized the name. Perhaps you'd like to help." Emily stood and rotated her shoulders. Being stooped over caused her some discomfort.

"Okay, what are the choices?"

"Right now, I have Top Dog, Bark in the Park and Dog Day Afternoon."

"Those are all good names, but does the charity event only benefit dogs?"

He had an excellent point. She shook her head.

"So maybe something like Paws for the Cause, Fur Festival, Pet Fest or Pet-A-Palooza?"

Emily dropped her shoulders. This guy was a genius. "I love those!"

He hung his head and blushed, showing Emily his shy side.

"Seriously, I'm using one of those. Which one I don't know. I think I'll let my boyfriend break the tie. That is if he's still my boyfriend."

The young man looked up. "I'm sure that if you were my girlfriend, any spat we had wouldn't last long." He dug his hands into his pocket and rocked on his heels.

"Well, thank you. I think I saw another side of you, and it's pretty cool." She flashed him a friendly smile.

After her scheduled appointments, she gathered up her stuff and headed back to the apartment. She called Connor to invite him to come over for dinner. One more day of delay to the printers would not be critical. It was important she let him weigh in on the name of the event since she'd asked him to help. Her call went to voice mail.

"I know you're probably on the set all day today, but why don't you come over later for dinner. Please. I have some exciting news."

She stopped at the store and bought items to make a

fresh salad, a loaf of sourdough bread, and one of those frozen lasagnas that actually tasted pretty good and cost less than if she made it from scratch. She had enough time to go over her business transactions for the month and get invoices ready to send out and fix dinner.

She chopped the cucumber, diced the onion, cut the green pepper into strips and tossed it with the lettuce. She'd preheated the oven, and when it beeped, set the lasagna inside. After spreading butter and sprinkling garlic salt on each slice of bread, she wrapped the loaf in foil and set it on the counter. She poured herself a glass of wine and sat. It wasn't like Connor not to call. She tried calling him again, but it went into his voice mail. Her second message came off sounding a bit more desperate.

"Hey, haven't heard back from you. The lasagna is in the oven. Should be done in about fifty minutes or so. Looking forward to seeing you. I've started on a glass of wine. Hurry over."

When another twenty minutes passed then ten more, she realized he wasn't coming. And not only wasn't he coming, he didn't even have the decency to call her and tell her why. She went to the kitchen and clicked off the timer. She'd lost her appetite.

Feeling a bit drowsy from the second glass of wine, she closed her eyes and fell asleep. The emotional roller coaster she'd been on with the charity event, and now Connor's behavior, had taken a toll.

"Don't," she mumbled, moving her hand away from something wet and cold.

A tug on her pant legs caused her to kick out. "Leave me alone," she whined.

She wrinkled her nose and sniffed. What was that

smell? Her eyes flew open. Daisy had her pant leg gripped between her teeth, and she was tugging with all her strength. It took Emily a few seconds to realize it wasn't a dream she was having; it was Daisy trying to alert her. The apartment was filled with smoke, and she began to cough. Then the smoke detectors went off, sending a piercing sound throughout the apartment. She grabbed her phone, picked up Daisy, and rushed to the front door. She barely got it opened before she fell ill by the inhalation of smoke. Coughing and spitting up, she made her way to the parking lot. She called 9-1-1 and reported the fire.

As a precaution, they insisted she go to the hospital. Inhaling smoke was nothing to fool around with. She called Kayla and asked her to come get Daisy from the neighbors before they whisked her off into the ambulance, sirens blazing.

After spending too many hours in the emergency room, she got the okay she could leave. Instead of bothering Kayla, she called Uber.

HOLDING HER HEAD, she cried. Kayla slipped her arm around her back to comfort her. "It's going to be okay, hon."

She reared up, her eyes likely red and swollen and her face blotchy from crying. "Now I need to add find a new home to my already growing list of things to do." She dropped her head into her hands and sobbed.

"You and Daisy can stay with me as long as you need."

"Thank you. I may have to take you up on your offer. Have you spoken with Connor?"

Kayla shook her head. "Voice mail."

Emily shrugged. "I tried calling twice. I got his voice mail each time, too. I know why he's not calling me back, but why not you?"

Shooting Emily a puzzled look, Kayla said, "Why wouldn't he call you?"

"We had an argument."

"Tsk. So what. An argument is no big thing."

"Apparently to your brother, it is." She leaned back, resting her head on the sofa back.

"I'll find out what's going on with him. I know he'd want to know about the fire."

"Well, it was more like smoke damage. Don't make it into something more than it was," Emily said.

"Whatever. The point is, you could have died!"

"Did the vet say anything about Daisy?"

"She said she was fine. Just keeping her overnight for observation. She saved your life, you know."

Emily nodded. "She's saved my life twice. First with the gunman and now this. How can I ever repay her?"

"With doggie treats, a warm bed, and lots of kisses," Kayla said.

"That's easy, but I'll ramp it up a bit."

Kayla patted her leg. "Everything is going to be all right."

CHAPTER 12

Connor practically broke down Kayla's door. He rushed to Emily's side and kneeled. "Emily, I heard. Are you all right?" He picked up her hand and held it firmly.

She slowly tipped her chin up and down. "Yes, I'm okay. I tried to call you. Why didn't you return my messages?"

"I lost my phone. I've been trying to retrace my steps to find it."

"Oh. Where did you find it at?"

"I'd left it at a bar the other night."

She pulled herself upright and straightened her torso. "Bar?"

"It doesn't matter now. All that matters is you're all right."

"I'm good. But why would you go to a bar?"

Kayla rushed in from the other room. "Emily, I heard back from the vet with an update. Daisy is doing fine and should be able to come home tomorrow morning." She flashed a smile toward Connor.

"That's great news, Emily. I was wondering about Daisy."

Emily pushed past Connor as she left him kneeling. "She alerted me to the danger. She saved my life again."

"She's one smart dog."

"I'm sort of tired, Kayla. I think I'll lay down in your guest room."

"Sure, hon. Go right ahead."

"Emily," Connor called out. "I'm glad you're okay. I don't know what I'd do if something happened to you."

Emily whirled around. "I hope you're being sincere, Connor. I had prepared dinner for us. I was excited to share some news with you, and you never called or came by. Now you tell me you lost your phone at some bar. I'm so confused. I need some time." She turned back around and made her way to the bedroom, leaving Connor and Kayla behind.

EMILY HAD A FRETFUL NIGHT. At one point, she had a bad dream, and in it, she heard the loud beeping noise of a smoke alarm and rose straight out of bed with her heart racing. She wiped away the sweat that beaded on her forehead and tried to go back to sleep.

In the morning, she staggered out to the kitchen where she found Kayla.

"Good morning, Emily. Coffee?"

"Yes."

Kayla jumped up and went to the cabinet. "Did you sleep well?"

"Not really."

"I'm sorry, hon. Maybe after you get Daisy this morning, things will feel better."

"I need to find a place to live."

"Emily, don't put that on yourself right away. I have plenty of space for you. One thing at a time." She set the cup of coffee in front of her.

"You're right. I have to call all my scheduled appointments and cancel them. I need to focus on the charity event. We're about thirty days out, and so many are counting on me."

"That's the way to go about it, Emily. One step, one day, at a time. First things first. Listen, I talked to Connor at length after you went to bed. He's so sad that you have this fight going on between you. He wants to make amends. He's sorry."

"I know. I'm being a witch, right?"

"No, I didn't say that. I think you were entitled to be angry with him, but he wasn't cheating on you if that's what you're thinking."

Emily stared at her, blinking a few times.

"I know you. I know us. We think that way and we shouldn't. Not all men cheat on their girlfriends after a tiny fight. Give Connor the benefit of the doubt."

"Why was he at a bar?"

"Probably getting his drink on. Probably bending the ear of the bartender. But he never even thought about being unfaithful. He cares about you."

"Thanks, Kayla."

"For what?"

"For being my friend. I needed to hear that. I'm glad it came from you."

"And it's not because he's my brother. If he behaved like a jerk, I'd say that too. No holding back the truth. But he is smitten with you. He cried and everything when he thought he'd messed things up."

Emily touched her heart with her palm. "That's so beautiful. I love a man who can show his emotions."

SHE DIDN'T HAVE to wait long for Connor to pound the pavement looking for her. He caught up with her at the veterinary clinic.

"Connor."

"I thought you might be here. Is Daisy ready to come home?"

"Yes. I'm waiting to go back and get her. I know she'll be so happy to see me. She hates kennels."

Connor sat next to her in the hard, plastic chair.

Emily sat with her hands clasped on her lap. Soon Connor rested his hand on hers. "I'm sorry, babe. Can we start over?"

She turned her head slightly, her eyes steady on his. "I'd like that."

His eyes never wavered from hers. She waited for him to reply, say something. Anything. He leaned over, brushing his lips across hers. Kissing her softly, she melted into him even more when a loud whoosh of air and noise startled them.

"Emily King?"

Emily stood.

"Daisy is ready to go home."

Emily held her hand out to Connor. He offered up the sexy grin she'd come to love, and the two entered through the doorway.

CHAPTER 13

With her hands crossed at her chest, Emily had watched as they hauled out her badly smoke-damaged furniture. Couch, mattresses, and anything that absorbed the nasty odor. She was forced to take all her clothes to the dry cleaners. Although once she saw the bill, she may have been better off buying all new clothes. Her wood furniture that wasn't sealed smelled of charred wood though no flames actually surfaced and had resulted in her buying new. Emily and Daisy had bunked with Kayla while new carpets, paint, and new appliances went in. She had a new apartment when it was all finished, right down to the mini blinds. Her apartment manager couldn't have been nicer about all of it. Said that's what insurance was for. His kindness took the pressure off Emily and allowed her to put the finishing touches to the Pet Fest, the name chosen for the event in between shopping for new furniture.

Emily and Connor held hands across the tabletop

before digging in. She'd invited him over for dinner to bless the new apartment.

"I'm so happy you're back in your place," he said, his eyes dancing in the dimly lit dining area.

"Me, too. I think Daisy is most happy about being back." She studied the little dog who appeared positively content in her sploot position, legs out, chin resting on the new springy carpet.

"Tell me how I can help with the Fest. What loose ends are dangling?" He released her hands.

"Help me direct."

He arched his brows. "Direct?"

"You know, be there when the porta potties get delivered, the canopies, tables, and booths. I have drawn up a plan of where things go." She slid back her chair.

She could feel Connor's gaze on her as she moved around the kitchen. She pulled up a drawer and retrieved a diagram.

"This is your copy." She dropped it on the table, and it pushed it toward him.

Picking it up, he examined it while sticking his fork into the tuna casserole.

"You've really thought this out." He let the paper fall to the table. "This was a huge undertaking. I hope the people who asked this of you realize it." He tipped his chin up and down a few times, then dug his fork back into the casserole. "By the way, this is delicious," he said.

"Glad you liked it. It's my mom's recipe."

"You can count on me and Kayla to help you with the Fest. I think it'll be a lot of fun."

"Thank you, Connor. You don't know what that means

to me." A small, secret smile pulled up on the corners of her mouth.

Changing the subject, Connor started telling Emily how things were going on the movie set. She hung on to his every word, not missing one detail. And even when it became a bit repetitious and boring, she never stopped paying attention.

"I don't know how you do it. All the retakes. I think about my clients, and if I ask them to do redo a pose, the reactions I get sometimes are less than favorable. Especially from children. I wonder how they get child actors to be so obeying?" She shrugged.

"Stage moms. They have a lot to do with how their kid behaves."

"You mean they yell at them?"

"Well, not always yell, but firmly tell them to get back in there and do the scene the way the director wants it. I've heard and seen a few tears shed. It's a little heartbreaking. I don't think I could do that to my kids."

"Me either. I can't even hardly discipline my dog." She pointed to Daisy, who now was tightly curled up like a donut, snoring softly.

"It gets weird. I walk off the set and go do something until they get it figured out. But there's this one teen, she's probably about fifteen. She's homeschooled on the set, doesn't have many friends, and I can tell she's not enjoying herself. She's there because her mom wants her to be."

"How sad. She should be out with her friends, at her own high school." Emily shook her head, trying to absorb the scenario of the teen.

"She's confided in me a few times. Said she doesn't really want to be an actress. She wants to be a veterinarian. She loves animals. We have a dog in the movie, and she spends a lot of time with it. Too much time. She gets yelled at for it." He chuckled.

"Maybe she'd like to come to the festival? There will be tons of dogs there!"

"I'll ask her. She might. That's if her mom will bring her."

"If she's as you described, a typical stage mom, she'll be there. Her mom would like nothing more than to rub elbows with all the money that will be there. And while she's doing that, we'll let—what's her name?"

"Lacy."

"Lacy visit the animals. I've already asked the shelters to have some of the dogs and cats that have been sheltered the longest to be there. We'll try to get them adopted."

Connor reared his head back and laughed. "Good luck with that. Her mom won't let her have one. Lacy told me she's already begged for a pet. Her mother supposedly has allergies."

"There's a solution for that. Some dogs are better for people who have allergies. Poodles for one."

"Emily King, you are one thoughtful person. I need you in my life."

"That's a strange thing to say." She could feel the heat travel to her face.

"In my line of business where I meet so many superficial people, people wanting something because they think they are entitled, I need a breath of fresh air like you to keep me grounded. You don't have a selfish bone in your body." He reached for her hands and held them, rubbing circles on her thumb with his.

Shivers ran down her back, and the knot that formed in her throat made it difficult to concentrate. "Connor, you're making me blush."

"I know. I can see those rosy cheeks. I'm sorry if I'm embarrassing you. I have to tell you how I feel."

"I'm glad you find many of my qualities endearing. I need you as well. You are my rock."

"Your rock? I don't know what I've done to deserve that, but it sounds impressive." He squeezed her hands.

"I know that you'll support me in anything I do. That's important." She tucked a loose strand of hair behind her ear.

He tilted his head slightly. Too sexy for his own good and making her pulse kick up a notch, she swallowed down that knot that came back while staying focused on his eyes.

"I think we are good together, Emily. I promise never to hurt you. I'll always be there for you. You can trust me and my word." He scooted his chair out and came around to her.

"I think I may be falling in love with you." He drew her up. Looping his arms around her, he held her steady.

The emotions that overcame him showed all over his face. His words rang in her head.

"I think I'm falling in love with you too," she said, aware her breathing was heavy and hung in the balance of this hot-blooded moment.

He pulled her flush to his body, his thumb brushing across her bottom lip. "You're so beautiful."

Fire ran through her veins. She craved him so badly. She posed for the kiss. The one she knew was coming.

The kiss started off soft but rapidly intensified as she held him, giving her an out-of-body experience she'd never felt before. And she never wanted it to end.

CHAPTER 14

A feeling of euphoria spread over her and through her like she'd never felt before. This man had such a hold of her heart, and she couldn't bear the thought of it ending. It would crush her. She knew that much. Love didn't come easy to her. Her parents always told her from the time she could remember that falling in love was forever, and waiting until the perfect man came along would be worth it. Sure, she'd dated. But no one made the earth move like Connor. This was for real, and she cherished every moment with him.

"Now that was a kiss," he said, holding her back and eyeing her up and down.

"Connor?"

"Yep," he said, still holding her.

"Have you ever fallen in love before?"

"Hmm."

"Either you have, or you haven't," she said matter-of-factly.

"True. I think I thought I loved someone before. But it turns out it was an infatuation."

"How'd you find this out? You know, that it was infatuation and not love."

"When she said she didn't love me anymore and it didn't really turn my world upside down like I think it should have."

"What about couples who go through a divorce. Sometimes they get to the end of their rope, and they're like ready for it to be over with. They loved each other at one time." She twisted her mouth as she pondered her own revelation.

"You have a point, but there are those couples who also can't let go even after the divorce. How do you explain that?"

"Denial. Scared of the reality." She shrugged.

"I know when she told me she wanted to break up, that it wasn't working, I felt relieved."

"If I told you it wasn't working, how'd you feel?" she asked.

He tugged at her shirt then pulled her close. "I'd stalk you until you changed your mind." He planted a kiss on her lips.

"Ha ha. A stalker, huh? That sounds interesting."

"I'm getting good practice. That's what I'm playing in the movie."

"You haven't talked about your movie much. I figured it was a big secret."

"Well, they don't want us telling too much. They want to sell you a ticket, but because you're dating one of the stars, you're going to get to see it before the public."

"How exciting!"

"Yes, I'm really digging my character. I will tell you that it is a thriller, and you aren't going to believe the ending."

"Connor," she said, slapping his chest. "You can't leave me hanging like that."

"Sorry. You'll have to wait until the end of November or so."

"It's a good thing I have the Pet Fest to keep me occupied."

"Speaking of…are you ready?"

"I'm as ready as I'll be. A week from Saturday. I hope you can break away from your rehearsal on Thursday and Friday. I really need you there to help me set it up."

"I already told the director that I need a few days off. He wasn't too happy about it, but since I'm one of the stars he's going to allow me a little freedom."

"Good."

"I had to use a little leverage. He recently gave someone time off for a baby, I figure this is your baby, so it was right up there with importance." He gave her a cheesy grin.

"Thank you." She slid her arms around him, resting her head on his chest. She drew in his scent while closing her eyes. She could hear the beating of his heart, and her breathing kept rhythm. Relaxing his hand on her head, he combed his fingers through her long dark hair while they held on tight. Yes, her parents were right. This was totally worth waiting for.

~

KEEPING your head out of the clouds when you were this in love was the hard part. She had a business to run, though, and keeping focused was literally harder than she expected.

"Please, you stand here, and hon," she said to the little girl with a flower in her hair, "come closer to your mom. Remember, you all are family and love each other. Say cheese!" She stepped back a few steps and clicked away.

She pulled in a breath and held it, letting it out slowly. Something was missing. "Just a second." She held up a finger and darted to the back room. Holding a large white stuffed dog, she held it out to the little girl. She then pulled two large wooden fruit crates from the other side of the room and placed them in position.

"Hon, you come sit here with the dog. Mom and Dad, you sit on the crates behind her."

Everyone did as they were told. Then Emily dropped a bright blue background down from her screens. The couple was dressed in blue and khaki while the little girl had a solid blue dress with a white flower in her hair. Satisfied it would make a cute picture, Emily shot away.

Her next appointment was a big star. In fact, so big he'd have bodyguards. Why on earth he chose her, she didn't know, but his money spent like everyone else's so she booked him.

She wiped her sweaty palms on a towel she kept nearby. She drank a full glass of water, trying to keep her dry mouth moist, but when he entered the room, she couldn't help but become starstruck. "Oh, he's gorgeous," she said under her breath.

She extended her hand. "Emily King."

"Chad Parker. It's nice to meet you. I've heard great things about you."

She cocked her head. She did a quick inventory of all her clients. Only one came close to his stardom, and she was retired. "Oh, by whom?"

"Connor Stone."

She drew her head back, her jaw gaping. "You know Connor?"

"Yes, we're making a film together. Didn't he tell you?"

"I knew he was making a film. I didn't know you were starring in it."

"Connor is starring in it. I'm supporting him."

Emily furrowed her brows. "He's the star, and you're the supporting actor? How does that happen?"

"The director saw Connor perform on stage back in New York. He's convinced that guy is going to be a household name someday. I'm there to help draw people to the box office."

"Name recognition?" Emily said, getting the space set up for his photo shoot.

"Yeppers. So, today I'm here for name recognition of a different sort. I know you've only started your business. Thought maybe I could give you a lift up. You know, get you some free publicity to grow your business." He smiled.

"That's very nice of you. Did Connor put you up to this because—"

He held up his hand. "No. I'm here on my own accord. I like Connor. I think he will go far. He is head over heels in love with you. This is my way of helping someone. One time someone helped me. Where shall I stand?"

Emily took a few headshots of the handsome guy as

well as a few full-length body photos. She had him do a few sexy photos too. I mean you can't have a photo shoot with Chad Parker and not include some with his sexy smile and dazzling eyes.

"Now that I've taken your pictures, what do you want me to do with them?"

"Send them to me. I'm going to get them out into the public. You wait and see. Soon you'll have people knocking down your door." He winked at her, making her grin.

"I'm already kind of busy."

"Yeah, taking family portraits. These people will be paying you big bucks. Wait and see."

"Speaking of big bucks, I'm organizing an event. It's for charity. To help sheltered pets. Would you consider being a donor?"

"Absolutely. Count me in for twenty-five thousand dollars."

Emily became speechless. She cleared her throat. "Thank you," she squeaked out.

Sitting on the couch with her legs curled up underneath, Emily held the phone to her ear and listened as Kayla went on and on about her new boyfriend, Spencer.

"He's such a gentleman. I've never had anyone be so kind and thoughtful."

"He's a keeper," Emily said, holding the remote and channel surfing.

"Did I tell you he bought me a dozen red roses?"

"Yes, three times." She clicked over to HGTV channel and watched someone paint cabinets.

"What about the dinner he fixed me?"

"Yep. Told me," she said.

"Sorry. I'm just so happy. I've never had—"

"A boyfriend be so kind and thoughtful," Emily finished her sentence.

They both laughed.

"Okay, so what's new with you and Connor?"

"Let's see. He said he thinks he's falling in love with me."

Kayla gasped. "Get out! Did he say that for real?"

"Yep. And I told him I think I'm falling in love with him."

"I'm so happy for you both. You guys are cute together."

"Also, has he told you anything about the movie they are shooting?"

"Not really. Said we'd be invited to a special showing. Why?"

"I had an interesting client today. Chad Parker."

"Chad Parker," Kayla screamed.

Emily held the phone out from her ear until her enthusiasm died down.

"Are you finished?"

"He is so adorable. How was he in person? Details. I want details," she repeated.

"He was very nice. Apparently, Connor sent him over."

"Connor? Our Connor knows Chad Parker?"

"They are starring in the movie together."

"What?"

"Yes, but get this. And you must pinky swear you won't tell anyone. And that includes Spencer."

"Okay. I promise."

"Connor is the star of the film. Chad is the supporting actor."

Another gasped floated through the earpiece.

"Connor told him about me and my photography business. He wanted to help me get discovered. He's going to purposely leak the photos out and give me credit for shooting them. And get this, he also donated twenty-five thousand dollars to the Pet Fest!"

"Emily, I'm so happy for you. Things are looking up, and it couldn't happen to a better person."

"Ah, Kayla, that's so sweet of you. I was going to say the same thing to you. I'm so happy you and Spencer have found each other. We must have another date night…and soon."

"You can count on us! By the way, Connor did mention the upcoming fest, and perhaps you could use a hand setting up. I'd like to volunteer our services."

"Thank you! I'll take you up on it. We'll be starting Thursday, finishing up on Friday and the gates open at eleven a.m. on Saturday."

THE QUIET ROOM SURROUNDED HER, and except for some paw licking by Daisy, she was alone with only her thoughts. It'd been a whirlwind ride since she left Texas. She recalled the day she drove away from her house, her parents standing at the end of the drive waving at her. She knew they didn't want her to go, but they also didn't want to stand in her way. She had dreams to pursue, and if things didn't work out, she could always come home. They couldn't understand what California could offer her that Texas didn't. But she had stars in her eyes and dreams filling her head of making it big someday with her mad photography skills. It didn't come out exactly the way she envisioned it, but it hadn't been a bad ride. She tilted her head back and rested it on the sofa, staring at the ceiling.

And now Connor Stone infiltrating her every being made the decision to move to California all that much more meaningful. A coy smile curled up at the corners of her mouth. Connor Stone and Emily King.

She let out a loud sigh as she gazed down at Daisy still grooming herself. "Daisy King, stop." Daisy looked up with her soulful eyes, blinked then resumed licking. Emily pulled up from the sofa and went over to the leash hanging on a hook nearby. She dangled it a few times to get Daisy's attention. Daisy leaped up and ran over, nudging it with her nose.

"Yeah, I thought that would get you up."

She hooked up her leash, and the two headed outside for some fresh air. The cooler temperature of fall felt good as they walked to the park. Moms with carriages sat on benches, chitchatting about daily things, and senior citizens shuffled and strolled the paved paths that meandered through the park. Dogs of various sizes walked on a leash, some with their noses to the ground, and others with their head raised proudly as they sniffed the air. Daisy, with her short little legs, jogged along, trying to keep up with Emily.

They'd rounded a corner when they heard the cry for help. Emily pulled Daisy along as fast as she could. Up ahead, Emily could see a small crowd gathering. She ran up to the people and squeezed between arms. There on the ground was an elderly man unconscious and what appeared to be his wife kneeling beside him, crying.

"What happened?" Emily looked for a response from anyone.

"He collapsed," a stranger yelled.

"We were walking, and he fainted," the older woman said.

"Has someone called 9-1-1?" Emily asked, trying to figure out what had happened.

"Yes, on their way," another stranger said, waving his cell phone around.

Emily leaned over the man with her cheek against his mouth. "He's breathing." She lifted his wrist, placing her thumb below his palm. "He has a pulse."

"Thank God," the older woman cried out.

Then the man opened his eyes and coughed.

"Peter!" the woman yelled. "Are you okay?"

He started to lift his head but quickly put it back on the ground. He made a few noises that told Emily he wasn't all right. "Sir, stay still. The ambulance is on the way."

The sirens could be heard in the distance, and soon the crew carrying a stretcher arrived.

Emily pulled Daisy out of the chaos and stood back, watching the medical staff work on the gentleman. Emily tapped a few bystanders on the shoulder, giving them the head motion to move back and let them work.

After they loaded him on the stretcher and most of the people moved away from the scene, Emily and Daisy walked up to the wife. "It looks like he's going to be okay. You should ride with him in the ambulance."

Clearly shaken by the incident, her hand trembled as she tried to make sense of it all.

"Ma'am, do you want to go to the hospital with him?" one of the crew asked.

"Is there someone I can call for you? Have them meet you there?" Emily asked.

"Yes, my daughter. I'm confused at this second. I can't remember her number. But it's under my contacts in my phone." She dug through her purse and handed Emily the phone.

Emily felt odd looking through the woman's contact list. "What's her name?"

"Jennifer Crowley."

Emily suddenly locked eyes with the woman. "Jennifer Crowley, the singer?"

"Yes."

"Ma'am we need to go now, please," the man in the dark blue uniform yelled out.

"She's coming," Emily called out. "Come on. Let's get you to the ambulance."

Emily quickly jotted down Jennifer's number while the medical crew helped Mrs. Crowley get settled in the ambulance. In a matter of seconds, the sirens blared and off they went, leaving Emily and Daisy standing on the curb.

She punched in her numbers and listened to it ring.

"Hello?"

"You don't know me, but I was walking in the park, and your dad collapsed. He's on the way to Mercy Hospital with your mom. I don't know any details, but he was conscious when they left the park. Your mom asked me to call you."

"What is your name?"

"I'm sorry, Emily King."

"Emily King, the photographer to the stars?"

Emily paused. "Photographer to the stars? I hadn't heard that one before, but yes, I do have a photography studio." Then her hand flew to her mouth to cover the gasp. "Do you know Chad Parker?"

"I'll fill you in later. Right now, I need to get to the hospital."

"Yes, and please let me know how your dad is."

CHAPTER 16

Soon after that brief call with Jennifer Crowley, Emily King became a household name—among the stars anyway. The requests for her services came barreling in at warp speed, and soon she had to turn people away. Famous people. People she'd only dreamed about gracing her studio with their presence let alone it becoming a reality.

"I need an assistant," she wailed over the phone to Kayla.

"That shouldn't be hard. There are people out there who would love a chance to work with you."

"This is crazy. This literally happened overnight. I can't even function right now. Do you realize within twenty-four hours my phone has literally blown up with requests? Chad wasn't kidding when he said he'd spread the news."

"You deserve it, Emily. We'll get through the charity event and tackle your overnight sensation, later." Her voice held a bit of royalty.

"Why thank you, Kayla," Emily responded with the same royal voice.

"Spencer and I are meeting you at the strawberry fields tomorrow, nine a.m. sharp."

"Good. I have Connor set up to help, as well."

"Anyone else helping besides us four?" Kayla asked.

"The company I hired for the canopies are setting those up as well as the stage and dance floor. The individual vendors are responsible for their own. We need to make sure everyone is following the diagram as to how it is to be set up."

"Got it. Well, I gotta run. See you tomorrow."

Emily returned as many of the calls she could, giving the short and sweet answer, "I'll get back to you," or "sorry, I'm booked into the future as far as I can see."

EMILY BROUGHT A LONG, soft kennel for Daisy. She knew it would be too long of a day for her to be hanging out, and it would keep her safe. She roamed around the grounds for a bit, but soon enough she crawled into her kennel with the soft sides and curled up for a snooze. Emily zippered her in so she could focus on what was going on with the setup, but she looked in on her from time to time, and if too much time lapsed, Daisy howled to let her know she wanted out.

Around five p.m., they stopped for the day. Exhausted, a bit dirty, and thirsty, the foursome gathered near their cars for a quick briefing on what to expect the following day.

"Tomorrow, the vendors show up. We'll direct them

based on the diagram. They all have a copy of it and know where they are to set up, but in case they need reminding," Emily said, tapping the document, "we have this. Any questions?"

Spencer raised his hand. "I imagine people will be bringing their dogs to this, right?"

"I hope so. It is a Pet Fest," Emily said, chuckling.

"What about poop. I bet there will be a lot of it."

"Good question. I should have thought of that. Hmm. I guess I'll see what I can do regarding that, but right off the top of my head I think we need some posts strategically placed around with some doggy bags attached, and a can nearby. Connor and I will stop at a lumber supply store and see what we can find. Thanks for bringing that to my attention, Spencer. Good teamwork."

He lifted his shoe and while balancing, turned it over. Everyone looked to the sole where dog poop was caked in the tread. "I figured since I stepped in some, it was the right time to bring it up."

Emily laughed so hard she grabbed her stomach, Kayla and Connor laughed so hard they began coughing, or more like choking, and Daisy began barking from all the commotion.

"What a way to end the day," Emily chortled.

"Hey, I aim to please," Spencer said, taking all the ribbing in jest.

EMILY LACED her fingers together as she held Connor around the neck. They gazed into each other's eyes then leaned in at the same time for the kiss.

"That's nice," she crooned.

"Glad you like it." His low, gravelly voice made the hairs on her arms stand.

"I'm sorry if I smell. It's been a long day." She shrugged.

"Can't smell any worse than me. I had fun working beside you." He kissed her again.

"Tomorrow we'll put the finishing touches, and Saturday, party!" She tilted her head back.

He kissed her neck while she was in that position. Then he trailed the kisses back up to her mouth. "Connor," she said through a whispered breath.

"Yes," he said, still kissing her.

"I'm so happy you came into my life."

He paused.

Something hit her she couldn't explain. Emotions were bouncing off of her like hail during a storm. She moved away and stared out the window.

He came up behind her, sliding his arms around her. "I'm ecstatic."

She whirled around to face him. "Really?"

"I told you. I'm falling in love with you. And after today, I can honestly say, I don't want to spend my life with anyone but you."

She raised up on her toes and kissed his warm lips. "I love you, Connor." She wrinkled up her nose.

"What's wrong?" he asked.

"I got a whiff of me. Phew."

"I love you stinky and all, but I think I'll let you shower and rest. Tomorrow is another big day. I have some lines I need to study too."

"Okay. Thanks for everything. See you tomorrow."

He left the apartment, but his earthy presence lingered, making her want him even more.

CHAPTER 17

 ven with the diagram, the vendors tried to be
sneaky. Emily and Connor were constantly
directing people where to put up their stalls. To break the
monotony, Connor and Spencer began playing inside the
jumping castle. Soon Kayla and Emily joined them. Four
adults acting like kids and Daisy barking at them nonstop,
running from side to side of the giant red and yellow
monster.

The girls tried out the wooden dance floor while
Connor and Spencer sang to them. Daisy tried to get in
on the act with her howling. Everyone fell out laughing.

"I think I'm delirious," Emily shouted. "The work has
fried my brain." She twirled Kayla around like a ballerina.

"I know, but it's been so much fun."

They moved on from the dance floor and stopped by
each vendor to see how they'd done and if they could
offer any assistance. They moseyed over to the food area
where the trucks were lined up, ready to serve up some
great grub.

"I'm so happy you went the food truck way," Kayla said, eyeing them.

"Me, too. It made sense. An outdoor fest, people and animals, I think it'll be great."

"And a variety too," Spencer chimed in.

"Something for everyone," Emily said, beaming.

"Let's finish up by placing those poop stations. Tomorrow is lights, camera, and action." Emily chuckled at her tie-in with all their professions.

Connor swung his arm around her and pulled her in. "If Chad Parker has anything to do with it, it'll be the event of the year."

Emily peered up at him, blinking a few times. "Yeah, I suppose so," she said under her breath.

EMILY FILLED the tub with warm water and set Daisy gently down. She squeezed some lavender dog shampoo into the palm of her hand, running it along Daisy's back, lathering the sweet-smelling soap, taking special care not to get any in her eyes. After a thorough rinse, she shampooed her one more time. Wrapping her in a towel, she patted her dry. Sitting cross-legged on the floor and cradling her in her lap, she turned her blow-dryer on low and dried her fur. Emily buried her nose in Daisy's fur. 'You smell so good, girl." Emily finished grooming Daisy by brushing her while they watched television. Daisy snored softly the rest of the night.

The following morning it was Emily's turn to get dolled up. She wanted to look nice because, after all, some prominent people would be attending. She selected a pair of slim-fitting jeans and a blue button-down three-quarter sleeve tunic. She slipped on a pair of dark blue loafers, added some simple jewelry, and brushed her long locks down, touching the ends up with a flat iron. Satisfied she was presentable enough for a good, fun-filled day in the sun, she slipped the new harness she'd purchased for this occasion over Daisy's head and waited for Connor to pick them up.

"Both you girls look stunning," Connor said, lowering his gaze to Daisy then back to Emily.

"Why, thank you. You're looking rather dashing yourself." She bent over, hitching the leash to Daisy's collar. "We're ready!"

When they arrived at the field once covered in rows of strawberries as far as the eye could see, but now covered in white-topped canopies, a red and yellow inflatable jumping castle, and a stage, it proved anything could be transformed with a vision and proper planning. They parked the car. People were already setting up their booths. In the distance, Emily could hear dogs barking. Daisy tugged at her leash, letting Emily know she wanted to go check out the commotion. Laughing, Emily let her lead the way.

The local shelter did a great job with their setup. Not only did they have enclosed tents, but they also ran portable air conditioning to ensure the dogs were comfortable. The high temperature was only to get to seventy-two, but the sun was beating down on the dusty fields.

"Hi," Emily said to the woman running the adoption tent.

"It's a beautiful day for a festival." She flashed a warm smile.

"Who did you bring with you today?" Emily motioned toward the dogs.

"I brought Lenny, who is a Jack Russell. He's about eight months old. Then we have Molly, the shepherd. She's about two years old." She walked over to the white curly dog. "This is Chrissy. She's a poodle and terrier mix. She's also about two years old. And lastly, we have Barnie. He's a seven-year-old dachshund. He's a total lover. I hope everyone finds a home today, but especially him. He's a senior, and it's been hard living at the shelter. His owner passed away, and the relatives dropped him off to us. He's a bit sad. They all want to go home with someone. That would be my wish." She reached down and patted Barnie on the head. Daisy kissed his ear and nuzzled his neck.

"That's my wish as well. I'll stop by periodically and see how you're doing."

The next stop she made was at the stage. The band was setting up. She located Jay and walked up to him. "Are you guys ready to rock it?"

"We sure are. We're totally pumped."

"I see you have a table set up with your CD for purchase. Great idea by the way." Emily crossed her arms.

"I thought so," Jay said, beaming as he puffed out his chest.

"Okay, well enjoy the fest. Remember to get some food and drink during your break and let them know it's on Emily King."

She caught up with Connor, Kayla, and Spencer who'd made themselves comfortable under the huge tent that had tables and chairs.

"You should see the cute animals up for adoption. I sure hope they find a home." She sat next to Connor.

He rested his hand on her knee. "Let's stay positive. With over three thousand people expected to visit today, and how many dogs are up for adoption?"

"Four."

"Four? I'm sure they'll find homes," he said, squeezing her knee.

"There's a senior dog over there that has had an especially difficult time. His owner passed away and left him with relatives who in turn gave him up. If something happens to me, please don't give Daisy to a shelter."

"First of all, nothing is going to happen to you, but if it did, I'd take Daisy in. Don't you worry about her. She's a great little girl."

"I think she felt sorry for old Barnie because he was the only one she gave any attention to."

"Dogs know when other dogs are sick or feeling blue," Spencer said.

"I've read that too," Kayla chimed in.

The group turned their attention to the shuffling of feet and noise. People were gathering and finding their way to the exhibits and booths. The band started up almost on cue, and soon the strawberry fields were alive with fest goers.

"Okay, everyone, this is where we split up. Mingle in with the crowds, be available if someone needs directions to the porta potties, food trucks, first aid station. Have your walkie-talkies on and your cells just in case. Let's meet back here in two hours," Emily said in her director's voice.

"You could be a director, you know?" Connor said, moving away from her. "Lights, camera, action," he said.

"Get out of here, Connor Stone. See you in two!" She pushed him away with a flippant wave of her hand.

Emily weaved her way through the crowds like a salmon swimming upstream. She found the two staffers overwhelmed at the ticket booth.

An entrance fee of fifty dollars a person would hopefully cut down the riffraff that might try to come in and spoil the fest. Anyone willing to shell out fifty bucks would most likely be upper crust as they say. One never knew, though.

"I imagine it will slow down some. Thanks for all your effort," Emily said.

After she left them, she headed over to the various booths and looked over what the vendors were selling. She stopped at the jewelry booth. After making small talk with the bubbly blonde, a pair of turquoise earrings caught her eye. "Can you save these for me?" She handed them to her.

"Sure."

"I don't want to be walking around with them. I'll come by before you close up."

The next booth she stopped at was the leather products. She drew in the rich, earthy smell of the belts and wallets. But the small crossover bag caught her eye. She took it down from the hook and looked it over front and back. "Good morning," she said, still holding the sweet bag in her hands. "Would you be able to hold this for me?"

He nodded, then ran his hand through his long, black beard.

"I don't want to carry it around with me. I'll stop by

before you close up. Have a great day," she said, handing the purse to him.

Emily stopped in front of the wooden sign vendor. Then a young lady ran up to her. "Are you working this event?" She clearly was out of breath.

"Yes, I'm Emily King. What's wrong?"

"My dog got away from me. I just turned around for a second."

Emily immediately recognized the young woman. She currently had a television show where she played a ditzy blonde. How ironic. "Okay, did you check the lost and found booth?"

"No. Where's that at?"

Emily held up her finger to the sign man. "I'll be back. I see something I have to have." She laced her arm with the woman's and quickly led her through the crowd to the lost and found.

As soon as they approached the tent, they could see a wagging tail.

"Pumpkin," she called, running up to the apricot-colored standard poodle.

"Glad she's safe," Emily said. She nodded to the lost and found workers and mouthed thank you. She was on a mission. A certain sign maker had caught her eye.

She narrowed right in on the wooden plaque. She had to have it.

"Can you please hold this for me?"

The older gentleman with a hearing aid smiled.

"Can you please hold this for me?" she said louder.

He came up and took it out of her hand. "Do you want to buy it?"

She cupped her hands around her mouth. "Please. Hold. It. For. Me," she shouted.

"Oh. Okay. It'll be right here." He slid it under a table in a box.

"Thank you," she mouthed to him.

She couldn't wait to hang the "This house is guarded by a corgi." And underneath the words, a corgi curled up in a donut. She laughed at her purchase. Her final stop for the day, gourmet dog biscuits. Baked by none other than a housewife from Hollywood Hills, married to one of the actors Connor knew. A line formed around the booth as people listened to her explain how the treats were made and with all-natural ingredients.

"Hi, Margo." Emily extended her hand.

"Emily King! So nice to see you."

"I see the people have really embraced the dog treats. I think I'll take two bags. One for Daisy and one for the shelter dogs."

"I've already delivered some over there. They loved them." Her eyes twinkled.

"Oh, great. Well then, I guess I'll shove off and let these people buy up the rest of your treats. Thanks again for supporting the Pet Fest."

Emily moved away, and soon several people took her place.

Next stop, food truck area. That was easy to find. She only had to follow the wonderful smells of garlic, chili pepper, and sugar. Someone walked past her with stuffed tacos in a paper tray that caught her eye. She saw kids eating cotton candy, and adults enjoying chicken on a stick. She'd looked away for a second. When she raised her head, there walking toward her was Chad Parker.

"Emily," he called out.

Emily smiled. Her gaze dropped to the two small children, each holding a hand. "Your children?"

"Yes. This is Parker, and this is Sadie."

"You named your child Parker?" She drew in her bottom lip after she realized what how corny it really sounded to have the same first and last name. Poor kid.

He moved in close. "It's one of those things we regret now, but he's five so kind of late."

"It's never too late for anything. What's his middle name?"

"Yeah, we thought about that, too, but it's another thing we regret. Anyway, how are things going?"

She started to open her mouth.

"By the looks of the crowd, I'd say it was a success." He flashed a toothy grin, touching the top of his daughter's head, her hair the color of summer wheat.

"Yes, the vendors have some great wares. I bought something from practically everyone. Now I'm checking out the food. The music is pretty good, too, for a no-name band."

"I hope the donations come pouring in."

"I'll head over to the donations booth soon and get a tally. We're taking all forms of payments. Cash, check, and credit card."

"No excuses not to give," Chad said. "Where's Connor?"

"We spread out. He's around here somewhere. Connor and his sister, Kayla, and Kayla's boyfriend Spencer. We also have about six other staffers roaming around. We can be identified with this," she said, pointing her chin down toward the paw pin and name tag.

"Good deal. Well, I promised the kids cotton candy and the jumping castle before we head out."

Twisting her torso back and forth, she sang out, "Don't forget to look at the adoptable pets. They are searching for homes."

"Daddy, can we?" the sweet little face with the hair the color of sun-drenched wheat said.

Chad furrowed his brows. "We've been over this. No time for pets. Let's hit the jumping castle. Bye, Emily."

"Bye, guys. Have fun." Shrugging, she said under her breath, "Can't blame a girl for trying."

After walking around the entire fest three times, it was time to meet up with the group. She pulled out a chair and dropped into it. Connor, then Kayla and Spencer showed up looking as beat as she. She patted the chair beside her. "Take a load off." Connor sat.

"Any worries?" she asked.

"Not really. I had to help someone over to the first aid booth. A bug bite that swelled up."

"I had to help the star of the television show Conquest find her lost dog."

"I saw her wandering around. No dog, though."

"Yeah, she turned around for just a minute," Emily said, mocking her.

She turned and looked over to Kayla and Spencer.

"Any concerns while you were out on duty?"

"No. Helped folks find the food truck, the potty; that sort of thing."

"Did anyone ask were the donation booth was located?" Emily addressed the whole group.

Everyone shook their head.

"So, either it was clearly marked, and they found their way there, or no one is donating."

"Now, Emily King, don't be a pessimist," Connor chided.

"Keeping it real. How about the adoptable pets? Have any of them found their forever homes?"

"Last time I walked by she still had the four, but several people were inside petting them," Kayla said.

"Emily, don't get any ideas. Daisy is enough," Connor said.

"Daisy! Oh jeez. I totally forgot about her."

"She's fine. She's enjoying being with the other dogs. I checked on her."

Emily stood. "Break time over with. I'm heading to two places. First, the donation tent then Daisy. I'll meet everyone back here in two hours."

CHAPTER 18

"What's the count for donations?" Emily peered over the shoulders of the volunteers.

"We're up to fifty-five thousand dollars," said the young guy with dark brown hair and glasses that seemed too large for his face.

Emily raised her brows. "That's great. We're only into the fest a couple of hours. By the end of the day, we should hit our goal of a hundred grand! Keep up the good work, guys. I'm headed over to the dog tent."

Daisy blinked her eyes a few times then slowly stretched out her legs, finally easing her way toward Emily. "Forgot about me that quick, huh?" Emily slipped her arms around her neck and gave her a hug.

"She's been such a sweetheart. She has taken a liking to old Barnie." The shelter worker nodded toward the dachshund who'd been sleeping on a mat near Daisy.

"I was hoping he'd get adopted by the time I made my rounds."

"Lots of people have been interested. Let's not count him out yet."

Emily looked around the tent. "Hey, wait. One is missing."

"Yes, Chrissy the poodle found her forever home." The gray-haired woman stared at Emily over her silver wire-rimmed glasses.

"I guess young and curly catches the eye first."

"I don't look at it that way. Certain dogs bond with certain people. They know who they like and want to go home with. The other dogs had their chance, but they didn't mesh."

"I guess so." Emily hung her head.

"We had a few interested in Daisy too." The woman chuckled.

Her head flung up as her pulse rocketed.

"Don't worry, I told them she was already taken. But let me tell you, that girl milked all the attention for what it's worth."

"I don't doubt that for a second. Are you getting any relief today so you can go and enjoy the festivities?"

The woman checked her watch. "Yes, in about fifteen minutes."

"Good. Remember, tell them your food and drink are on me."

"Thank you!"

"I'm off for another round. See you later." Emily reached down and patted Daisy on the head. "See you in a little while."

During her stroll through the fest, she encountered a vendor yelling at a potential buyer.

"Can I assist you in some way?" Emily crossed her

arms, her gaze darting from the man behind the booth and the woman shaking her fist.

"I bought this. I mean, I literally just bought this. It's empty!" The woman held out a bottle of aromatic oil.

"She's lying. She bought it about twenty minutes ago. Enough time to dump the contents into her own bottle."

"That's absurd! I would never do such a thing."

Emily watched the back and forth drama play out. Finally, she intervened. "Listen, I don't know who is telling the truth or who is lying. We're all adults here, though. So how shall we handle this?"

The man relaxed his agitated stance, and the woman flexed her hand and dropped it to her side. "I don't know," the man said through gritted teeth.

Emily's gaze dropped to the large handbag the woman was carrying. She caught a glimpse of a dark brown bottle. The kind used for oils. She cleared her throat. "Did you buy more than one bottle from him today?" She tilted her head and narrowed her eyes.

"No, she only bought the one," the man said, speaking for her.

"What's that?" Emily pointed into the bag.

The woman clutched it closed. "What?"

"I saw what appeared to be a brown bottle. Like the one you have in your hand. Let us see it."

"Never mind." Tossing the empty bottle at the man, she whirled around, brushing past Emily, and while dodging the crowd, escaped quickly out of their sight.

"I told you she was lying." The man held up the empty bottle.

Emily mumbled sorry, then headed through the crowd. She hoped that person left the fest.

"Lady, can you help me find my mother?" Brown doe-like eyes blinked back tears.

"Sure, honey. Where did you last see her?"

"She left me over there." The little boy pointed to a bench. "Said she'd be back. That was a long time ago. I'm scared. Where's my mommy," he wailed.

"Okay, dear. Let's go to the lost and found. Maybe she's there."

As they walked along, she encouraged the little boy to look around. "If you see her, point her out," Emily said.

"Take your hands off of my boy!" a woman screamed.

Emily jumped back. "He was lost. He was scared."

"I told you to stay put. I'd be back." She grabbed the boy by the hand.

"Hey, that's not really necessary, is it? He was scared."

"Mind your own business."

"Now just a minute." Emily looked over the crowd to see if she could locate the security personnel they'd hired. She kept one hand on the walkie-talkie button. She'd call if she had to.

The woman's eyes narrowed, focusing on Emily's name tag. Her judgmental glare made Emily feel small and insecure.

"Emily King? Founder and organizer?" The woman raised her brows to her hairline.

"Yes, that's me," she said, patting her name tag.

The woman put out her hand. "I'm Patricia Clark."

Emily looked away. *Why did that name sound familiar?*

"Maybe you don't know me, but I own the restaurant downtown, The Black Tie."

Emily snapped her fingers. "Yes, I know of that restaurant."

"Anyway, I did not abandon my child. I was looking at some of the booths, and he was complaining he was hungry and tired. I gave him a drink, some food and told him to sit there. Maybe the time got away from me, and I left him there too long. But I did not in any way leave my child stranded."

"Of course not, Ms. Clark. There's no need to explain yourself. The important thing is you have been reunited. Enjoy the rest of your time here. And, Ms. Clark?" Emily stood steadfast, her voice strong and steady.

The woman arched one brow.

"Don't forget to make your way over to the donation booth. They'd love to record a large donation from you." Emily grinned as she walked off but not before flashing a tiny smile to the little boy.

"Well I never. I suppose you are bribing me."

Emily kept walking and never turned around.

STANDING in line waiting for food, Emily noticed a few famous people. A few spoke, but for the most part, people went about their business supporting the event.

"I'll take a fish taco and a bottled water, please," Emily said.

After she got her order, she found a bench and devoured her food. She didn't realize how hungry she was. A shrill noise, followed by a scream, made her look up. A circle formed near her, and the sounds of flesh on flesh made her nauseous. She ran over to the crowd while asking for help on her walkie-talkie. In a matter of a few minutes, the hired security was breaking up a fight.

Bloodied noses, cut knuckles oozing in blood, and two fat lips, the young men who got into it—over a girl—were handcuffed and detained until the city cops came.

The girl, sobbing into her hands was what Texas girls called, a hot mess. With black mascara smeared all over, her eyes red and swollen, the girl tried to tell Emily what had happened.

Who were these people, Emily wondered?

"Listen, I don't know who you are, but if I were you, I steer clear of those guys. They aren't worth it. Find yourself a good guy. Despite the tale, they aren't that hard to find."

"They are the twin sons of Clarence Brothers."

Clarence Brothers, a director known all over L.A. In fact, he was directing Connor's movie. Emily took a deep breath. "Okay. So, they are the sons of someone famous. And who are you?"

"I'm the daughter of the maid who cleans their house."

"You can do better than them. Trust me. They don't deserve you." Emily tossed her arm around her. "Why don't you call a friend and get a lift home. Those two are going to jail."

Emily watched as the girl stood to the side and called someone on her cell. Feeling a bit emotional over the whole thing, she made her way back to the dogs for some furry love.

Daisy and Barnie were snuggled together on the mat. "Oh boy. These two are becoming fast friends."

"Yep. And guess what? Molly found a home!"

"Who?"

"One of the security guards here. We're holding her until he gets off."

"That's great news. Now we just have Lenny and Barnie to place," Emily said, tipping her head.

The woman checked her watch. "We have plenty of time. We'll be loading up in about three hours. The dogs can't stay much longer than that. But we'll leave a sign up with information in the place of the booth for the duration of the fest if that's all right?"

"If that's all right? Of course, it is. This is a Pet Fest, after all. I think I'll take Daisy with me to the big tent for a while." She reached down and leashed her up. Daisy wouldn't budge. "Come on, girl. Let's go see Connor and the gang." She still wouldn't budge.

"I'm afraid she doesn't want to leave Barnie," the woman said.

"I see that. But at some point, she's got to."

The older woman shrugged.

EMILY FOUND THE BIG TENT, entering it from the side. She looked around until she found Connor.

"There you are. We were getting worried about you," Kayla said.

"You won't believe what I've been through. A lost boy, and a fight."

"Did the lost boy find his mom or dad?" Kayla asked.

"Sort of. I was walking him to the lost and found booth when she came out of nowhere yelling and accusing me of practically kidnapping him!"

The group gasped and made a few other expletives.

"But I fixed her. I basically told her we'd be expecting a big donation from her in order to keep my mouth shut about her unfounded accusations. But never mind her. Then a fight broke out between twin brothers."

"Over a girl and alcohol was involved, right?" Spencer cut in.

"Over a girl. But I don't think any drinking was involved. But who knows. I called security, and the city cops hauled them away."

"And the girl?" Kayla asked.

"The daughter of the housekeeper for the boys' family."

"Who were the boys' family?" Connor asked.

"You might want to sit down for this," Emily said, biting her bottom lip.

CHAPTER 19

Connor listened, then drew in a big breath and let it out loudly. "The good thing is the boys got taken away before they put it all together and the girl, she'll probably not remember your name. We're good," he said.

"What kind of young men is this Clarence Brothers raising? Fighting like dogs in the street. They were a mess, blood dripping from everywhere."

"I'm not worried about how Clarence raises his kids."

"But I do have some very good news," she said.

All eyes and ears were on her.

"Two of the dogs have been adopted!"

Kayla clapped. "I already knew that. I was keeping it a secret." She laughed.

"And Daisy wouldn't leave Barnie's side. I might have to adopt him."

Connor gaffed. "You need another dog like you need another hole in your head."

"Don't be mean, Connor. Barnie is missing his family. He's scared and alone. Daisy has really taken to him."

Connor raised his hand and swatted the air. "Do what you want. You will anyway." He winked.

"I'm waiting. But I wish someone would take him home. Lenny is still there, too. Kayla, you need a little dog. Lenny is energetic, sweet, and would make a good watchdog." Emily moseyed up to her and swung her arm around her shoulders, trying to butter her up. "Poor little Lenny." She puckered out her bottom lip.

"Emily King?"

The foursome looked over to where the voice came from.

There standing with Jennifer Crowley was the older woman whose husband had fainted in the park.

Emily moved forward. "Mrs. Crowley. How is your husband doing?" Emily rested her hand on hers.

"He's doing well. It was his blood sugar."

"Dad is a bit stubborn when it comes to his diabetes," Jennifer said.

"I'm happy he's doing well. Did you just arrive at the fest? Oh, how rude of me. These are my friends, Kayla and Spencer and Connor."

Jennifer nodded; Mrs. Crowley smiled.

"We've been here for a while. The music is pretty good."

"Yes, they aren't bad. They're not Jennifer Crowley though." She giggled.

"We stopped by the donation booth. I gave them the check I promised you."

"Thank you so much."

"It was my pleasure. Anyway, I'm going to hit the food trucks before I go get Barnie."

"Barnie!"

"Mother is adopting him."

"You don't know how happy that makes me. He's such a sweet little dog."

"A little corgi seems to be attached to him. I hope she finds a home soon."

Emily giggled. "That corgi …she belongs to me. She is there keeping Barnie company."

"Oh good," Jennifer said. "It was nice meeting you all. Have a great rest of your afternoon." She held up a quick wave.

"I'm so happy right now, I could dance. Barnie is getting the best home."

Connor frowned.

"What's wrong. Don't you approve of them?"

"No, I think they'll be a great family for Barnie. I'm trying to figure out when we dropped back to being friends."

Kayla and Spencer made a quick getaway, leaving them alone.

"Connor…"

He turned away from her to be dramatic.

"I know you aren't really mad."

"And how do you know that?"

"Because." She leaned over and whispered something in his ear.

He pulled her toward him and planted a kiss squarely on her mouth.

"Connor Stone. See. I knew you weren't upset with me."

"Hey, you two lovebirds!"

Emily and Connor jumped when they saw Lyra St. Claire.

"Lyra," Connor said. "So nice to see you."

"Yes, nice and surprised," Emily said.

"I noticed online one of the vendors was going to have gourmet dog treats. Cinnamon loves homemade baked goodies."

"Margo is selling them like hotcakes. You better hurry."

"Good," she said, rocking back on her heels. She turned and began to walk away, then suddenly stopped. "By the way, that band is pretty good for a garage band." She winked, then with a swoosh of her flowing dress in vivid colors of orange and yellow, she was off again.

"I admire her so much," Emily said, her gaze following Lyra as far as she could see.

"She's wonderful," Connor echoed as he put his arm around Emily.

As the two lovebirds stared off into the crowds of people, a familiar face came into view. Connor moved away from Emily and stepped forward with his hand extended.

"Chris!" The two shook hands.

Emily's eyes grew big. Swoon-worthy Chris Ryan entered her personal space. She blinked a few times and clasped her hands in front.

"This is my girlfriend and best photographer in the world, Emily King."

"Nice to meet you finally. He talks about you nonstop." He elbowed Connor then laughed.

"I'm such a big fan of yours."

"Good. Glad to hear that. Listen, I came by because my word is my word. I want to leave this with you." He handed a check to Emily.

Emily swallowed down the lump that tried to take up residence in her throat. "Gosh, Chris. This is so nice of you." Her bottom lid began to fill with tears. "I'm sorry about the tears. It's so thoughtful of you." She wiped the few strays that trailed down her cheek.

"No worries. I can't stay, but looks like a nice crowd came out to support your cause."

"Thanks, man." Connor reached out and shook his hand and with his other, rested it on Chris's shoulder. "See you soon."

"Oh, and that band. It's really good. I don't think I've ever heard of them before."

"Jay's Garage Band," Emily said, a cheesy smile curling up on the corners of her mouth.

He gave them a backhanded wave, and off he went, deep into the sea of people.

Emily folded the check and slipped it into her pocket.

"Come on. Let's get out of here and go listen to some music and kick up our heels a little. I think we've earned a little bit of fun." Emily grabbed his hand and led the way out of the tent.

Jay's Garage Band strummed out the last chord to a song, and the crowd broke out in applause. The few people on the dance floor shuffled off, waiting for the next song to start. Connor and Emily found a couple of empty seats and sat. Soon the band started again, and the same few people made their way back onto the rented dance floor, bopping their heads, swaying their hips, and getting into the beat of the song.

Raising his voice slightly, he said, "They're pretty good." He tipped his chin.

She pointed to the table that held the CDs for sale. "Earlier the table was full. They've sold quite a few."

Without any notice, Connor stepped over to the table, picked up one of the CD jewel cases, and turned it over. He reached into his pocket, retrieving some bills and pressed them down into the plastic container overflowing with money.

"Here. Don't say I never buy you anything." He handed her the CD case.

"Ha ha." She playfully bumped shoulders with him.

"Thanks, everyone, for coming out today and supporting the Pet Fest. Emily King has done a great job organizing this, don't you think?"

The crowd erupted in applause.

If past occurrences told Emily anything, she was quite sure her face had turned two shades of deep red.

"So, this song's for you, Emily," Jay said into the mic. "We wrote this song when were about seventeen years old. It's been sitting on a shelf getting old and dusty. We've cleaned it up a bit, and I think it's fitting for today. Here we go." He looked back at the rest of the band as he strummed out the first chord. Soon the rest of the band joined in, with Jay leading the vocals.

It took a few times for the chorus to sink in, but when it did, Emily's pulse kicked up a notch, her palms grew sweaty, and she became so aware of Connor sitting next to her it almost overwhelmed her. Her knee pressed up against his and feeling him near her gave new meaning to the song as Jay belted out the tune. Suddenly, Connor reached over and grabbed her hand, placing their laced fingers more on his leg than hers. Shivers ran up and down her back.

"Would you like to dance?"

She didn't answer him but instead nodded. He pulled her up, and like a sheep, she followed him out to the dance floor. He whirled around and pulled her in. She closed her eyes and breathed him in before melting into him. The song brought so much emotion not only to the floor but to them. His hands rested above her hips, and as they moved to one of the most beautiful songs she'd ever heard, she gave her heart, along with a lifetime of commitment to him at that very moment. At the Pet Fest. On a Saturday evening. She laid her head on his shoulder as she shuffled her feet to the prettiest love song ever.

When the song ended, she held him tightly for a few more seconds. Letting go right now seemed premature. She wasn't ready.

"That was my favorite song of theirs. I hope it's on the CD." She rocked back into his strong arms and studied his profound and alluring expression. Her gaze darted to every part of his handsome face from the cute dimple on his chin and the five o'clock shadow, to his piercing blue eyes.

"I really liked it, too. The lyrics were so heartfelt, and the melody…it gave me chills."

"Hey," she said.

He lowered his gaze.

"Thank you for letting me be me."

He chuckled. "Who else would you be? Are you one of those people with a split personality?" He held her out, his neck scrunched in as he inspected her.

"No, that's not what I meant. I feel so free to be me when I'm around you. That's hard to do out here in la-la land." She smiled.

"I get it." He reeled her into his arms and hugged her. "I feel the exact same way." He kissed the top of her head.

"Two more hours and it's a done deal. Let's go grab some chicken skewers and some lumpia. I'm starving,"

Talking about food may have broken the romantic hold for a moment, but Emily definitely would revisit it later.

Holding a paper tray with half a dozen lumpia fried to golden-brown perfection and chicken on a stick, the couple weaved in and out of the remaining crowd which by any standards, was still quite a few, people watching as they devoured their late-night snack.

"The people out here are so interesting," Emily said, tipping her head to the lady with long, flowing hair the color of purple, wearing a one-piece leotard in leopard print.

"I know what you mean. But to be fair, every state has its exceptions," Connor said, choosing his words wisely.

"I like the way you say that. Exceptions. That's a nice way of saying—"

"Weird," they said in unison, breaking out in fun-loving amusement of their timing.

"I need to go get Daisy. The shelter folks will be closing down shortly."

They picked up their pace and made it time. The woman's worried look told Emily she'd cut it a bit tight on picking up Daisy.

"There you are. I was going to have the Garage Band

make an announcement." She handed over Daisy's leash, with Daisy attached to it.

"I'm sorry. The time got away from me. I hope she wasn't too much of a bother."

"No, she was fine, but all the dogs got adopted, and she felt a bit lonely, I think." The woman dropped her gaze to Daisy.

"I'm so happy they all got adopted. I was worried about the little bouncy Jack Russell."

"He went to the perfect family. They have a huge yard for him."

"Listen," Connor said, breaking the ice. "I'd like to make a one-time donation to the shelter." He pulled out his wallet.

"Oh, how nice of you," the woman said, changing her tone from slightly irritated to joyful.

He leafed through the bills and pulled out three one-hundred-dollar bills. "You do take cash, right?" he said, holding them out to her.

The woman took the money out of his hands. "Of course."

"Thanks again for being part of the fest. Do you need any help?" Emily offered.

"No, we got it. I'm leaving our sign up. If you can take it with you tonight and drop it by the shelter one day, that would be most helpful."

"Absolutely," Emily said.

Connor and Emily, along with Daisy, started to walk away when the woman called out.

"She's had dinner, by the way."

Emily lowered her gaze to Daisy. "Thank you," she mouthed.

"What's wrong?" Connor asked.

"You don't know much about dogs, do you?"

He shook his head. "Not really. Just what I've learned by watching you with Daisy."

"Let's say, it may be a long night for both Daisy and me." She let out the deep breath she held.

Shrugging and with a look of total confusion, Connor caught up with Emily and Daisy as they made their way to the donation booth.

"Okay, how are we doing?" Emily looked over the shoulders of the volunteers.

"Busting it wide open," one of the takers said with a grin.

"Good. That's what I want to hear. This gig is about done."

"So far, we're sitting at two hundred thousand dollars and some change."

"What? We climbed that much since the last time I checked?"

"Huge donations came in from a few people."

"Well, I have one more big check to add." She pulled out the check from Chris Ryan and handed it over.

"This is going to bump it up," one of the trusted and thoroughly vetted volunteers said.

Emily took her phone out and stared at the screen. "Forty minutes left. I'm going to have Jay make an announcement and see if we can't get a few stragglers to toss a few coins in the jar. Some may feel pretty generous with their pledges after visiting the ice cream truck."

The truck made the most delicious ice cream sundaes using alcohol. And for the folks under twenty-one, an alcohol-free version. Connor and she had shared a chocolate bliss, and it was scrumptious. If the frozen alcohol treat wasn't enough, the margarita truck offered another type of sinful pleasure. It came in traditional lime, strawberry, and one she wasn't too sure about, coconut.

"Come on. Let's see if we can encourage a few more donors." Emily hurried toward the stage. When she was able to get Jay's attention, he strolled to the end of the stage and leaned over.

"We're about to wrap this thing up. Can you please let folks know if they haven't had a chance to donate, now is the time?"

"Sure. Anything for you." He stepped back and moved to the center. Holding the mic firmly, he spoke to the crowd. "Hey, guys. It's been a blast performing for you all today, and into the night. We hope you've enjoyed your time here at the first annual Pet Fest! Be sure to visit the donation booth on your way out, and so you all remember what this shindig is about, this song should remind you." He turned, giving the nod to his band, and on the count of three, they busted out in their version of "Who Let the Dogs Out."

Emily eyed the crowd. A lot of head bopping and foot stomping ensued by the energized song, but then slowly, a few at first, then several more headed toward the donation booth. After Jay and the band sang through the lyrics a few times, only a half dozen or so people stood.

"Thanks for coming out." Jay strummed the last chord for the night, leaving only the sounds of a few remaining people scattering about the strawberry fields.

The volunteers who had been running the donation booth handed over the two large green bank bags. "Here's the checks."

Emily held them tightly in her hands.

"And this is all the pledges. Has their name, phone, email, and the amount pledged. We told them someone would be contacting them within the next few days." Another volunteer handed over a black zippered bag.

"And this…is the donation jar."

"It's pretty hefty. Did anyone count it?" Emily's eyes darted from one volunteer to another.

"Yes, I did. There's about five hundred dollars."

"Okay, and the ticket master at the front entrance sold fifteen hundred tickets. So at fifty dollars a head that comes to…"

Connor whipped out his phone and moved his fingers around the screen. "Seventy-five thousand dollars!"

"This has been a total success," Emily yelled.

"Let's get this money to the bank," Connor said. "Makes me nervous to be carrying this much around."

"Remember, your girlfriend has mad martial arts skills." Emily posed her hands in a deadly move.

Connor stepped back and hugged his arms. "I'm definitely scared of you!"

Connor, Kayla, Spencer, and Emily, along with one tired Daisy, stood and looked at the dusty fields that just a couple hours before had white tents, booths, crowds of people, and food trucks. Seeing the empty fields signified the day was done and time to go home and rest.

As they headed back to the cars, Daisy stopped dead in her tracks and wouldn't budge. She pulled Emily in another direction. With her nose to the ground, she began sniffing.

"Hey, Connor. This is what happens when dogs get

strange food before it is appropriately introduced to their diet."

Daisy squatted.

"Eww, gross," Connor said.

Emily shrugged. And in the back, Kayla and Spencer emitted more adjectives befitting the matter.

CHAPTER 20

"Can I tell you without a doubt, what we just shared has brought us closer together?" His sarcasm rang throughout the sentence and made Emily shoot him a look.

"Ha ha," she bantered.

Connor raced off down the road, breaking a few speed limits. He got them home safe but just in the nick of time. Poor Daisy.

"I'll boil some chicken and rice. It helps soothe the stomach. If that doesn't help, canned pumpkin."

"I won't stay. Plus, it's been a long day. It's after midnight. I hope you two get some rest." Connor bent down and petted Daisy. "Sorry girl. Hope you feel better." Just then, her tummy rumbled so loud even Connor heard it.

With a tone of emergency, Emily said, "Stand back. Things are about to get messy."

Connor bolted straight up and took a few steps back. "Night all," he said, moving away and toward his car.

"Sure. Abandon me in my time of need."

"I'll stay if you want me to."

"I could use some help boiling the chicken and rice."

"You got it. I'm here for you."

WHILE EMILY repeatedly and hurriedly took Daisy outside, Connor boiled chicken and rice and made sure Daisy had plenty of fresh water. He was a fast study. Emily was happy he decided to stick around.

Exhausted from so many bathroom trots, Daisy finally curled up in a donut and fell asleep.

"I think we may be through the crisis," Emily said, leaning her head back on the couch.

He pulled her close and kissed her. "I had a great time today. You totally knocked it out of the park. People are going to be asking for your help all the time."

"I can't do that. I have a photography business to run."

"Maybe once a year? I think the Pet Fest was a hit. I, for one, loved the non-black tie event."

He stood and stretched. "Gotta hit the hay. I have an eight a.m. screen call."

She walked him to the door. "Thanks again for everything. I couldn't have done it without you." She raised up on her tiptoes and kissed his nose, then his mouth.

When she began to lower her feet, he pulled her up and brushed his soft lips across hers.

"Well," she said, a coy smile sweeping across her mouth. "That's the way I want all my days to end."

"If you stay with me, I promise they will." He kissed

her one last time, flipped up his hand in a wave and out the door he went.

She held the door snugly as she watched him get in the car and drive away. Once inside with her back up against the door, looking at a peaceful Daisy, she mumbled under her breath, "Connor Stone. I promise."

SHE VISITED the bank first thing to deposit the proceeds but kept the rest of her schedule clear for a couple of days. Between Daisy getting the loosey-goosies and Emily's sheer exhaustion from the event, she not only needed, she required, some serious downtime.

Now that fall was officially here, Emily longed for some fall temperatures to go along with it, but one thing she learned living in Southern California, there only seemed to be a steady temperature of mid-seventies, sunshine, and if they were truly lucky, a sprinkle or two of rain. And with fall not only were temperatures supposed to be crisp but holidays were around the corner, and nothing said holiday more than Emily's mom's stuffed bird and homemade pies. *Wonder if Connor would be willing to go home with me.*

It felt good to lounge around in her yoga pants and a long tee shirt with Daisy curled up at her feet. Channel surfing, reading and relaxing for two days felt amazing, and when she went back to work shooting pictures of week-old infants, generational photos, engagement and now, because of the recent magazine article about the Pet Fest and how much money was raised, weddings! Realizing she was not superwoman no matter how many times Kayla told her she was, she placed an ad for a couple of helpers.

She got a few hits with her brief but to the point ad. She set up interviews for later in the week starting with the one she felt would be less suitable and saving her favorite for the last. So she could remember him. His credentials were fabulous. He'd worked with some legit studios with big names.

But things didn't always work out the way you think they will. Turned out, Mr. Credentials was nothing but an overinflated ego, thinking he was everyone's gift. Emily could barely get through the interview. She shook his hand and told him she'd be in contact, but the truth of the matter was, as soon as he left, she shredded his application, sprayed Lysol all over the room to disinfect and rid it of his overbearing ego, and moved on with the second interview.

She was cheerful, outgoing, and cute as a button. Those weren't Emily's words. That's how her grandma would have described her. Emily saw her as an over-achiever, confident, and attractive. But could she take pictures?

"On your application, you state you've never been paid for your photography."

"Yes, that's true. It started as a hobby." Her gaze never wavered from Emily's.

"That's always good when you can turn a hobby into a paid profession. That's sort of how I got started. I took photography in school. My teacher gave me the confidence to come out to California and see if I had what it took to make it."

"Apparently, you do." Her tone was clear, her words precise.

Emily leafed through her portfolio she'd brought to the interview. Many of the pictures were excellent. The kind that told a story. And they say a picture is worth a thousand words or something like that. That was impressive for sure.

"Sara Beth, is there anything else you'd like to add?"

"No. I need this job. I hope you'll consider giving me an opportunity."

Emily knitted her brows. Need this job. That seemed kind of odd coming from someone so confident as herself.

"I'll make my decision soon." She stood and extended her hand.

Sara Beth had a firm grip.

The last but not least...the one she knew for sure would be the best candidate turned out to be worse than Mr. Big Head himself. How could that be? Because a few answered questions online do not make for a proper first impression, that's why.

She sat back in her swivel chair, tapping her chin with the eraser of her pencil. She drew a big X over Mr. Big Head's name and the last interviewee. It looked like Ms. Confidence would get the job. Emily hoped they would get along.

She called Sara Beth with the good news. She accepted the offer and agreed to start the following Monday. Emily warned her about the heavy schedule. "I'm booked solid for several months out, and I don't see it letting up anytime soon."

"That's good. I like to keep busy."

"Listen, I had a hard time getting hold of your references. Do you have someone else you'd like to list?"

Sara Beth gave her a couple more names and numbers. She called the first one.

"Hello, my name is Emily King. Sara Beth Johnson has applied for a job as a photographer for my studio. She listed you as a reference."

"She learned the skill while incarcerated, waiting for parole," the voice said.

Emily's chin dropped. "Oh. I didn't know that. She forgot to mention that part to me."

"She wasn't in for some heinous crime. She wrote a bad check."

"Ah, I see. Uh-huh. Okay. No worries. I understand."

"She was between a rock and a hard place. She's got mouths to feed. Her husband left her. She did what any mom would do to take care of her kids." The woman's voice, not defensive, came over loud and clear.

"I'm not judging. She seemed like a great person. Very confident. I wished she'd divulged that little bit of information instead of me finding out like I did."

"She's not proud of it. It's hard for her to discuss it. She lost her kids to the system anyway, even after she tried to do her best to keep the family together. Now they don't want anything to do with her. It's a sad situation." The woman softened her voice, and it compelled Emily to respond.

"I'm not a mother, but I can only imagine. Thanks for the info."

"Emily Stone?"

"Yes?"

"Please give her a chance. She really needs this job."

Emily drew in a deep breath and paused before letting it out slowly.

"I haven't made my decision yet. I'll let her know one way or another."

"Thank you, Emily."

Click.

Pause.

"In prison!"

THE WHITE CARDBOARD boxes with the metal hangers lined up on the counter were oozing with wonderful smells. Chinese food always tasted best when lounging in yoga pants and long tee shirts.

Armed with chopsticks and napkins, Emily and Connor sat on the couch sharing food and details of their day. When Emily told him about Sara Beth, his chin almost hit the floor.

"Seriously? Prison, huh?"

"Yep. But it's not like she committed murder. She wrote a hot check. To feed her kids." Emily stuck the chopsticks inside one of the containers and produced a piece of chicken dripping in thick red spicy sauce. She popped it into her mouth and chewed.

"Did you like her overall?" Connor peeked inside the container and stabbed a piece of chicken, bringing it up to his mouth.

"Yes. I felt she would be the best of the three."

"Then go with your gut, but hide the silver." He winked then let out a small, raspy laugh.

CHAPTER 21

Sara Beth arrived a few minutes early. Being late was a pet peeve of Emily's. Sara Beth made brownie points.

"Good morning," Emily said as she uncoiled the cord to the vacuum.

"Good morning."

"So each morning I run the vacuum, dust, and make sure the studio is tidy. Then, I go through all my screens to make sure they roll down and back up without any issues, check over my props, and that sort of thing." Gripping the handle to the cleaner, she rolled it over to Sara Beth and handed it over to her. Sara took it and smiled.

"While you're spiffing up the place, I'm going to do some recordkeeping. I usually do it at night, but things have been pretty hectic."

Sara Beth located an outlet, plugged it in and soon the humming and vibration of the machine echoed within the high ceiling space.

Emily popped open her laptop, pulled up a stool to

the long, flat desk, and began to look her account over. Every so often she'd check on Sara Beth. She trusted her for the most part, but it was like any new working relationship. Testing the waters was the only way to know for sure.

"Where can I find a dusting wand?"

Emily looked up. "In that other room." She slipped off the stool. "I realized I have not given you a proper tour. Follow me," she said, motioning to Sara Beth.

"This space could be made into a studio apartment. Right now, it has a small galley kitchen and a bathroom and a couple of storage closets." Her voice echoed in the room. "Daisy stays back here sometimes and sleeps." Their gazes lowered to the fluffy dog bed with Daisy in it, looking at them with sleepy eyes. "It's a little early for her still." Emily giggled. "I keep all the cleaning stuff in this closet." She opened the door nearest to them.

Sara Beth took a few steps toward the closet, taking inventory of the items. She reached in and grabbed the dusting wand, some rags, and some all-purpose cleaner. "I saw a few smudges." She held up the spray cleaner.

"Very good. So anytime you want to make a cup of tea or put your lunch in the fridge, you're welcome to come in here."

Sara Beth did a great job with sprucing up the place. More brownie points. And when she asked her to retrieve certain props during the shoots, she was Johnny-on-the-spot. Emily made up her mind that after lunch, she would let her do some photography.

"Let's take a lunch break. We've got three more clients coming this afternoon. Thought maybe you'd like to take the pictures." Emily arched her brows.

"That would be awesome. I'm kind of nervous with you around, but I'll do my best."

"Don't be nervous. I don't bite. I'm here to help you." Emily entered the room where the kitchen was. She came out with her half a tuna sandwich and a salad she'd painstakingly prepared the night before, adding bacon bits, black olives, and even a separate baggie for her croutons. She plopped down on a stool where the once desk now became a lunch table and began to open the container with her salad.

"That looks yummy."

Emily's gaze lifted from her salad to the saltine cracker Sara Beth was about to put in her mouth. Then she lowered her gaze to the plastic bag of grapes.

"That's your lunch? Saltines and grapes?"

"I eat light."

Sara Beth's face turned several shades of pink. Was she telling her the truth? "I have more salad then I need. Let me get you a bowl." She slid off the stool.

"No, that's fine, Emily. You don't need to share your food with me."

Emily stopped. She slowly turned toward Sara Beth. "Tell me, do you eat crackers for lunch because you really want to, or are you eating them because you can buy a whole box of them for a dollar at the dollar store?" Her gaze scanned Sara Beth for the truth.

Sara Beth hung her head and stared at her meager lunch.

"It's okay to not have funds for certain things. There's no shame in asking for a little help."

"I've been out of prison for seven months. This is my

first job opportunity. I rent a room, walk, or take the bus, and yes, I'm a frequent shopper at the dollar store."

Emily paused. Blinking back tears, the emotions overcame her quickly. She hurried to Sara Beth and hugged her. She felt cold and stiff. Emily wouldn't let go of her until she relaxed and hugged her back. Pushing back slightly, Emily studied her face. "Don't be too proud to ask for help. You've paid the price for your wrong. Now it's time to move forward. I'll help you in any way I can. But you must let me know what I can do."

"Giving me this job has helped. After a few paychecks, maybe I can move out of the hotel and into an actual apartment."

"That's the spirit. Baby steps," Emily said, her words resonating with encouragement.

Sara Beth tucked a few strands of hair behind her ear. Her eyes began to fill with tears. "My children don't want anything to do with me. They're embarrassed by me." She wiped the tears that fell down her cheek.

"Maybe in time," Emily said, offering a speck of hope to an uncertain outcome.

"I doubt it. Their father has turned them against me." She wailed into her cupped hands.

Emily rushed to her and held her. Patting her back, she let her cry.

"I'm sorry. I should be stronger than this." She searched the room for something.

Emily took the cue and ran for the box of tissue. Handing her the entire box, she stood back with her arms crossed. "I know I'm outside looking in, but I also know that time heals most wounds. Your ex-husband can't be that much of an ogre to keep the children from you. He'll eventually see that doesn't do you or them any good. Kids need their moms too."

"I hope you're right."

"How old are they, and what are their names?" Emily sat and took a bite of her sandwich.

Sara Beth's eyes lit up, and soon she couldn't stop talking.

And the brownie points kept adding up. Emily smiled as she slid over her bowl of salad and offered Sara Beth a plastic fork.

EMILY STOOD BACK with her arms crossed as she watched Sara Beth make her way around the studio. She was a natural. She checked the lighting, made sure the props showed well in the lens and gave the clients wonderful instruction on where to place their hands and feet.

"Emily, please take a look at this." Sara Beth stepped away from the camera so Emily could take a look at the scene.

"Looks great. It will be a great shot. Go for it."

"Thank you, Emily and Sara Beth," Kayla said.

Emily swung her arm around Kayla. "Now tell me again…what are these pictures for?"

"It's our anniversary pictures." Kayla flashed a warm grin over to Spencer.

"Anniversary? You've only been together for like six months or so." Emily tapped her finger to her chin.

"I know, but when you have some great moments, you have to record them, right?" Kayla shrugged.

Emily arched a single brow. Was Kayla up to something else? "If you say so." She pulled her out of earshot of Sara Beth and Spencer.

"Give it to me straight. You didn't come to get anniversary pictures."

"Spencer asked me to marry him," she whispered.

Emily gasped. "What? So, these aren't anniversary pictures."

Kayla shook her head.

At the same time, they squealed, "Engagement pictures."

"I haven't told Connor yet, so mum's the word."

"Sure. That's not for me to tell him. When is the wedding?"

"We haven't really set a date. We don't want to rush into anything."

"Listen, while I have you here. I've been thinking about asking Connor if he'd like to go to Texas with me for Thanksgiving. Do you think it's too early to meet the parents and all of that?"

"I think he'd go. He's in between jobs so he'll be on vacation for a while. Yeah, I think it's a great idea."

"I bet he's exhausted with back-to-back movies."

"He really is. He said having two come out within a few weeks of each other is crazy. He's hoping for good feedback," Kayla said.

"Let me know once you tell him. I hate keeping secrets from him."

Emily and Sara Beth waved to them as they exited the studio.

"Your best friend?" Sara Beth asked.

"Yes. I'm with her brother, Connor."

"I see." Sara Beth began to tidy up the area for the next clients.

Taking pictures with dogs and kids could be a challenge, but when you had subjects like Corky the corgi and darling children such as Isabelle and Marc, and just as wonderful parents, Corrine and Luther, well nothing could ever go wrong.

Daisy and Corky had been running around the studio playing. They were besties from a long way back, and whenever Corky came to visit, Daisy and he would tear up the place. The good thing about it all was it tired out Corky so much that he would behave for the pictures. But Sara Beth still had her hands full. But when she finally found the perfect shot, she clicked away.

Emily stood back and watched while Sara Beth did her thing. She was pretty awesome to watch. She had such patience with the dog and the children. She had a wonderful gift, and Emily was excited to have her join her growing business.

After the last client left for the day, Emily asked her how she felt.

"Tired, but in a good way. It has been a terrific first day."

"Good, I'm glad you feel that way. I have to tell you, watching you from a distance, you have a really good eye for detail. You'll make a great photographer."

"Thank you. Coming from you, I take that as such a compliment."

"Does that mean you'll be coming back tomorrow. For more of the same?" She hunched her shoulders and raised her brows.

"Yes. I'll be here. Bright and early." Sara Beth reached

out and rested her hand on Emily's arm. "Thanks for the pep talk today during lunch."

"You're more than welcome. I can't predict the future, none of us can, but if you keep working hard and don't take your eye off the prize, I think you'll see your kids soon."

The corners of Sara Beth's mouth curled up. She nodded, then grabbed her few personal items and headed out.

Emily lowered her head and stared at the floor. A colorful little bobble caught her eye. She moved to it and picked it up. Something one of the children left behind. She squeezed the pink and blue little beads into her palm as she contemplated her strategy to help Sara Beth.

It wasn't too difficult to find Sara Beth's ex-husband. Several articles mentioned him. Because the children were minors, their names were never disclosed. She found a phone number for him and called. Her heart raced as it rang. When a man answered, she almost hung up. Maybe she'd overstepped the bounds of boss and employee, although she felt more of a kindred friendship with Sara Beth.

The man repeated hello.

"Yes, hi. I'm Emily King. I own a photography studio in L.A."

"And you've employed my ex-wife and want me to help how?" His sarcasm and anger drilled into her ear.

"I don't really need any help. And how did you know I've employed her?"

"Because I have an investigator following her every move. I don't want her anywhere near my kids."

"Isn't that against the law? I mean to follow someone around who hasn't done anything wrong? That, to me, borders on harassment." Emily dished some of the same anger back at him.

"She's done plenty wrong."

"She's paid the price too."

"Listen here, Emily King. I don't need a lecture from you."

"I'm not lecturing you, but merely giving you a piece of my mind. Sara Beth has served her time, and yet, you and I'm sure many others in society will continue to make her a prisoner. She would like to see her children. They are not just yours!"

"Well, that isn't going to happen. They don't want to see her anyway."

"That's because you've painted a bad picture of her to them. Admit it. You were angry, embarrassed and you took it out on Sara Beth by corrupting the innocent little minds of your children. You disgust me."

"I don't care if I disgust you. You have no idea how hard it has been." His tone softened a tad, and Emily wondered if it was enough to wiggle through and talk some sense into his thick skull.

"I can't imagine. But Sara Beth loves those children. She's doing her best to prove to you and to the world she's to be forgiven. Please. I'm begging you. If you have an ounce of humanity, a speck of common decency, please at least consider letting her see them in the future. You have time to make it right. You can start by having a conversation with your children."

"I'm not promising anything."

"At least you're not saying no," Emily spoke softly.

"Listen, don't call me again. If I'm interested in doing what you suggested, I'll call you."

"Fair enough. I won't bother you again. And hey, if I catch your investigator snooping around my place, I'm calling the cops. I'm a law-abiding citizen, and I won't be treated disrespectfully by you or anyone else. Got it?" She clicked the phone and dropped it on the table before he could answer. She meant what she said.

She moved to the kitchen and poured herself a glass of wine. She might have nerves of steel and a few krav maga moves under her belt, but she still could get rattled by men who were insensitive. Connor wasn't like that at all, and she was so happy about that, too.

Thinking about him made her want to hear his voice.

"I so needed to hear your voice," she said, closing her eyes. "It's been one heck of a day."

"How'd things work out with Sara Beth?"

"Fantastic. She's awesome. So patient, detail oriented. I made the best selection when I hired her."

"Good. Glad to hear it. You sound dejected, though. I can hear it in your voice."

"No, not dejected. Sad a little. Sara Beth's ex-husband won't let her see the kids. He's still punishing her."

"What a jerk."

"That's what I said. So, I called him tonight to see if I could open his heart a little to the idea."

"Gosh, Emily. Not sure that was wise."

Emily sat straight up. "Why?" She held the wineglass to her lips.

"You're interfering with someone's decision, and it involves their family, children specifically. Not sure you should get involved."

"If you could have seen the look on her face when she talked about them, the bucket of tears she shed today over not seeing them, perhaps you'd feel differently. I'm rather surprised by your reaction."

"I don't think something as sensitive as a family member should be discussed with an employer."

"You've never talked about anything personal to your director, or coaching staff, or whatever you call people in the movie industry?"

"Yes, I have, but I hope you haven't!"

"What?"

"It would be like you calling my director and discussing something personal with them behind my back."

"I got it now. So as long as I don't show any signs of caring, I'm okay. But hold the line if I do care to cross it? That's ludicrous."

"Emily, I didn't mean it like that. But we're not married."

"No, we sure aren't. That's for sure. Listen, I've got to run. Someone who cares needs me."

"Emily—"

Click.

She sat back and took a sip of her wine. She shook her head. Taking another sip of her wine, she played over in her mind the argument they'd had. Was she out of line? Her phone started ringing. It was Connor.

"I guess you had more to say?" She jabbed at him some more.

"You hung up on me, remember? I still had plenty to say. This argument is silly. I don't want you getting hurt. I know your heart is in the right place."

"You do?"

"Of course, Emily. That's why I love you so much. You

are always thinking about others. It doesn't surprise me at all you want to help Sara Beth. Just be cautious."

"I'm sorry," she blurted.

"For what?"

"For being short-tempered. It is something I need to work on."

"I don't want you to change a thing about you. I love everything about you."

"I wanted to ask you something," Emily said.

"Go ahead."

"Would you like to come to Texas with me and have Thanksgiving dinner with my family?"

"Meet the parents?" he bellowed.

"That too."

"Of course. I'm on hiatus until I can pick up another acting job. But I don't mind the vacation. It's been a brutal year with two movies at once."

"I know, Connor, but how exciting too."

"We got word that Jackson's Rage won't be out until spring, but they're pushing hard for a Christmas Day release of Fools Fall in Love."

"Coming to Texas won't ruin anything?"

"Nope. If they get confirmation of a Christmas Day release, we'll have an early screening, but probably won't be on Thanksgiving Day. Besides, I want to meet these King parents."

"I'm going to get Sara Beth up and running to handle everything while I'm gone. I'll schedule real light the couple of days before the holiday. I was thinking we'd fly up on Wednesday and come back on Friday or Saturday. Kayla isn't going home until Christmas, so she's going to watch Daisy for me."

"Sounds like you have it all planned. I'm in. I'm one hundred percent in."

"Thanks for calling me back and clearing the air. I hate to go to bed angry."

"Talk to you soon. Love you," Connor crooned into the phone.

"Love you too."

Click.

Emily held the phone for a moment. Her eyelids filled with tears. It'd been one emotional day. "Come on, Daisy girl. Time to hit the hay." She swallowed down the last sip of wine. Carrying her glass to the kitchen, she carefully rinsed it out and set it in the dish drain. A warm feeling washed over her, no doubt from the wine. She'd sleep like a baby.

OVER THE COURSE of the next couple of weeks, Emily showed the ropes to Sara Beth on every aspect of photography she could think of. Sara Beth already knew a lot. She seemed to be enjoying working at the studio, and Emily kept on adding up the brownie points.

"Connor and I are heading to Texas for a few days for Thanksgiving."

"Will the studio be closed?" Sara Beth asked.

"I'm going to have a light schedule for you on Wednesday. It's mainly Christmas card shoots. It happens at this time every year, people wait until the last minute. I think we have three scheduled for the Wednesday before. I think you can handle it."

"Yes, no worries."

"Then we'll open back up on Friday, and I have only one scheduled. Most people will be out shopping for Black Friday."

"And Saturday?"

"Two for the morning. I'll be home late Saturday. We're closed Sunday and back open on Monday. But it's going to be kind of light through the end of the year. Come the first of the year, busy again."

"What about Daisy?"

"Kayla volunteered to watch her. Do you have any plans for Thanksgiving Day?"

"My sister and brother-in-law invited me over. We're trying to put the pieces back to our relationship. It's been slow," she said.

"The important thing is it's moving in the right direction," Emily said.

"I wish I could see my girls. But I know that won't happen."

"Sara Beth, it may. Give it more time. Enjoy your celebration with your sister. Remember, baby steps."

She nodded.

"Okay, let's get back to work, shall we?" Emily moved to the screens and pulled down the winter scene for the next shoot. "This is a popular one for Christmas cards."

"You have my number and Kayla's. If you should need anything, don't hesitate to call."

"Sounds good. You guys have a great time in Texas." Sara Beth pulled Emily in for a hug.

"I hope you have a blessed holiday with your family.

Take care." Emily whisked around, grabbing Daisy's leash and her roller bag. She didn't want Sara Beth to see the tears. She gave her a backhanded wave, and off she went.

While on the drive over to Kayla's, she gave Daisy a pep talk too. Seemed she was rather good at these. "You be a good girl for Kayla." She roughed up her fur and scratched her behind the ears, making her yawn.

After she dropped her off, she headed over to Connor's place. She parked her car, and they used a paid car service to get a lift to the airport.

They made it to the airport where the waiting began. Shuffling in the long line of security, they moved at a slow pace, pulling along their carry-on baggage.

"You're not nervous, are you?" She laced her arm with his.

"Not in the least, why?"

"Meeting the parents is a big step in our relationship." She hugged his arm close to her body. "I promise they don't bite, and Daddy won't meet you at the door with a barrel staring you down in the face." She laughed.

"That's good to know." He rested his hand on hers and held her arm in his.

"I hope you like country cooking. My mom is the best."

"I love food in general. You know that." His eyes twinkled as he dropped a kiss to her forehead.

They got through the line without incident before more waiting.

"This is what I hate about traveling. All the waiting. Not to mention the drive to LAX." She leafed through a magazine.

"For a two-hour flight, no less."

"I think I'd like to live in a small community someday.

Get out of the rat race," she said, still looking at the magazine.

"You mean a house on a tree-lined street with a white picket fence?" He playfully knocked shoulders with her.

"Maybe." She rolled her head toward him and smiled.

"I like that idea. Maybe a few kids and of course, some dogs."

"It's getting better all the time."

An announcement came they'd be boarding soon.

"I'll make one last trip to the bathroom." She jumped up and tossed the magazine on the seat.

Connor laughed. "I'll be right here waiting."

The plane was full of holiday travelers. Some were stopping in Dallas, and others had connecting flights out. Emily's parents lived about an hour outside Dallas, and with all the traffic lately, it took closer to two sometimes. She could hear her daddy now. His frustration about all the growth. He'd never survive in L.A.

They made their way to the passenger pickup area. The exit doors slid open with a whoosh as they moved through it with their luggage in tow. Emily located her dad and rushed toward the truck.

A big barrel of a guy ran toward her, scooping her up and twirling her around. "Emily, my baby girl. So good to see you."

"Daddy, this is Connor," Emily said, throwing her arms open toward him.

"Nice to meet you, sir," Connor said.

"Good to meet you, Son. Call me Walt. Well, let's hit the road. This darn traffic is a nightmare. Who in their right mind would live in this," he said, his voice trailing off as he lifted their baggage into the bed of the truck." Hop in, kids. Your momma is waiting."

Emily could see out of the corner of her eye, Connor sizing up her father. When she caught him staring, he tried to cover up by nonchalantly looking out the side window.

Her dad talked nonstop, and it helped to make the almost two-hour drive go fast. Emily shoved Connor out of the car so she could hug her mother, who was standing on the porch waving.

"Momma," Emily said, wrapped in her arms.

"Come on, Son. They'll be there for a spell." Emily's dad opened the squeaky screen door and motioned for him to enter. The old door bounced a couple of times before it rested.

"It's so good to see you, dear," Emily's momma said.

"I can smell the home cooking out here!"

"I've tried to make all your favorites. Let's go inside so I can meet your new fella."

When the ladies entered the cozy kitchen with the bright yellow walls, Connor and her daddy were sitting at a farm-style kitchen table, drinking iced tea.

"Did you offer the boy anything to eat?" Emily's momma asked, rushing toward the counter where she exposed a big plate of homemade chocolate chip cookies.

Emily laughed when she saw Connor's eyes widen to the size of the plate.

"Help yourself, Son."

"Momma, this is Connor."

"I know it is, silly. And I'm Emily's momma. You can call me Rebecca." A low belly roar shook her apron and the plate she held out.

She pulled out a chair and tipped her head for Emily to join them. "I want to hear all about those movie stars you get to rub elbows with." She leaned in, resting her chin on the palms of her hands, her brown eyes, same as Emily's, blinking while he tried to swallow his bite of cookie.

"Momma is excited because she heard you were making a movie." Emily reached for a cookie, plopping it straight into her mouth. She palmed her stomach. "These are so delicious."

With his mouth full, Connor agreed.

After the small get-to-know-you around the table took place, Emily decided Connor had been through quite enough of the "parents" and told her momma and daddy she was going to show him around.

"That's good, dear. Supper will be around six. I hope you like liver and onions."

Connor, tongue-tied and not sure how to respond, nodded instead.

Emily laughed so hard her side started to hurt. "Connor, you have to learn when my momma is kidding. She's not making liver for dinner. What are you making, though?" She cocked her head, tears of laughter riding on her lower lid.

"Thought we'd have something on the light side. Tacos."

"Momma's tacos are anything but on the light side." Emily laced her arm in Connor's. "But they are really good." She looked back over her shoulder. "We'll be back in a while."

"Have fun. Don't do anything I wouldn't do," her momma called.

Connor cut his gaze to Emily, then a small smile crossed his face. "Another joke, right?"

"Connor, don't be so sensitive. Let's go check out the farm."

They walked around to the back of the house where the barns, stables, and huge garden were.

"What kind of livestock does your parents' farm have?"

"Pigs, a few sheep, a couple of horses, an old milk cow. We had more, but it's hard for them to keep it all up. They have fifty acres."

"Fifty acres!"

Emily lifted the large black metal lever that held the barn doors closed and swung it to the other side. Immediately, the smell of hay and animal smells smacked them in the face. Emily took in a deep breath. "I love the smell of the farm. Animal poop and all." She grabbed a pitchfork.

He furrowed his brows, unsure of what she was going to do with the weapon she held.

"We use this to get the hay and toss it into the pens."

She walked over to one of the pens where two pigs were sleeping. "These guys were little piglets the last time I saw them."

Connor peered over the enclosure. Two large pigs huddled in the corner.

She carried the fork over to another pen where an old mare stood. "She's still hanging in here. I used to ride her when I was younger." She opened the gate and stepped inside, adding some fresh hay. "See that grain over there." She motioned with her chin to a sack.

He nodded.

"Grab a scoop or two and put it in that bucket and bring it here."

He did as he was told.

"Now gently offer her the bucket and see if she'll eat some."

He did as she said. The old mare nudged his hand first, then stuck her nuzzle inside the feed bucket. "This is awesome."

After they spent a little time in the barn, they held hands and walked through the woods. They crossed a small footbridge with gurgling water. The green ferns and other plants landscaped the slopes of the creek, and as dusk fell, the woods became quieter and darker, and a bit spookier. For Connor.

"I think we should be getting back," he said, trying to keep the worry from his voice.

"You're not scared, are you? I used to roam these woods even in the dark. I did carry a flashlight, though. Yes, let's get back. I can smell the liver a mile away."

"Liver! Thought she said tacos. Liver was a joke?"

"Connor Stone. I know you're not that gullible. Yes, tacos. Scrumptious tacos you've never tasted the likes of before." She squeezed his hand.

When she felt him pull her back, she turned her body slightly. "What's wrong?"

"I know once we get back inside, I won't be able to do this." He reeled her in close to him and brushed his lips across her mouth. She released his hand and pulled her arms up around his neck, kissing him deeper. They stood in the woods holding on tight, and the only sounds were the occasional falling twig from the huge trees or the squeal or chirp of a creature that called the woods their home.

"I see where you get your beautiful olive complexion

and deep brown eyes. You're the spitting image of your momma."

"Why, thank you. I'll take that as a compliment."

"And you got your daddy's sense of humor."

She laughed. "I do."

"So, what's their story?" he asked.

"Story?"

"How'd your parents meet?"

"Momma's parents came here from Israel. She went to college at the University of Texas, but she fell in love with a certain star running back and well, the rest is history.

"Did she finish college?"

"Yes, but barely. Right after graduation, they got married. My grandparents bought this land and gave it to them as a wedding present."

"Wow. That was very generous of them."

"Back then, land was a lot cheaper, but it was still a substantial gift."

"Your grandparents?"

"Gone. Grandmother died about five years ago and Grandfather two years ago."

"Did they live with your parents?"

"No, they had a little cottage down the road." She looked off toward a gravel road. "I'll take you to it tomorrow."

They stopped short of the back door. "Connor, if you can remember this, you'll be fine with them." She nodded to the door. "Daddy is a big jokester, but so is Momma. They play off of each other too. So look to me, and I'll guide you through it all. But they are sweet people, and I know their heart is in the right place. I can tell they already love you."

"And that, my dear, you got from both of them." He pulled her close and tapped a light kiss to her forehead.

～

"Aunt Macy and Uncle Tony are coming tomorrow as well as your cousins, Cory and Bella," Emily's momma said. "Bella got married last year." She glanced at Connor.

"Momma, I know. Remember, I was in the wedding." Emily scooped some ground beef into a shell and topped it with shredded cheese.

"So, honey, are you really making a living out there in California?" Her daddy's gruff Texas drawl stole the conversation right out from under Momma.

"Daddy, I am. I haven't had to ask for any money, have I?"

"She's successful," Connor interjected.

"She could have been successful here. They offered her a job." Her daddy chomped on a crisp taco shell; pieces shattered onto his plate.

A look of confusion spread across Connor's face.

"Teaching photography to high school students," Emily said.

"An honorable position, wouldn't you say, Connor?" Her dad's gaze stayed steady on his, making Emily came to the rescue.

"Dad, leave Connor out of this. He is a guest."

"What's done is done, dear," Emily's momma said, changing the trajectory of the conversation.

Emily sighed. "Thank you. I love what I'm doing."

Connor leaped back into the deep waters. "She hired a helper. And someone who needed the job." Connor tipped his chin, encouraging Emily to tell them about Sara Beth.

Emily's eyes grew wide, and she shook her head.

"Oh?" her dad said.

"It's nothing really." She reached over, squeezing Connor's leg.

After she managed to escape the questions regarding Sara Beth, she helped her mom clear the table. Her dad asked Connor to join him out back for a cigar. Emily mouthed to him to let her dad do all the talking as they headed to the large screened porch.

"I really like Connor. He's so handsome," Emily's mom said as she filled up the sink with water.

Emily opened the cabinet under the sink and retrieved the dish soap. "I'm glad you like him because I love him." She tossed the silverware into the sudsy water.

"Love?"

"It doesn't mean we're getting married or anything. It means we've taken our relationship to the next level."

"I'm so happy for you, dear." Her voice appeared strained.

"Are you? Happy for us?" Emily stood back and studied her mom.

"I'm a little sad too. You live so far away. I miss you."

Emily hung her head. When she raised up, she saw tears in her mom's eyes. "Mom. It's okay. I can visit you often, and you can get on a plane, too, ya know." She reached out and patted her arm.

"We need some help out here," her dad yelled.

Emily dropped the sponge, and with suds flying every-where, ran outside with her mom behind her.

Connor was stooped over retching.

"What happened?" Emily shot a wicked look toward her dad.

"I don't know. One minute we were chatting and smoking cigars, and the next thing I knew, he was turning all shades of green, ran out to the yard and started puking."

"Was it my tacos?" Emily's mom cried.

Emily rolled her head toward her mom. "Really, Momma? Tacos" She shook her head. "Connor, what do you need?"

He gave her a backhanded wave.

"Let's go inside you guys. Give him some privacy."

She ushered her folks inside. Her dad commented as he entered through the threshold. "You should have seen him, Rebecca. He turned every shade of green."

"Daddy!" Emily said.

AFTER ABOUT THIRTY MINUTES, Emily checked on Connor. He'd moved from the bushes where he'd tossed his tacos to the screened porch. He rocked softly as he stared out into the dark woods.

"Sorry," he whispered.

She sat in the chair next to him and began to rock. "It's okay. You haven't smoked a cigar before, have you?" She rolled her head, studying his profile.

"Yes, I have. But nothing as strong as those stogies." He chuckled.

"I'm glad you're feeling better."

"I bet your daddy thinks I'm a total loser."

"Why? Because you couldn't hang with him smoking

cigars?" She shook her head. "That's plain stupid. Of course, he doesn't think that. Now Momma, on the other hand..."

Connor cut her a wild-eyed look.

" Kidding." She held out her hand.

He laced his fingers with hers as they rocked in silence with only the occasional hoot of the night owl letting them know they weren't the only ones out tonight.

"How'd you two sleep?" Rebecca asked as she poured them each a steaming cup of coffee.

"Momma, that old mattress needs to be tossed out. It's too lumpy." Emily rubbed her backside.

"Noted." She stood at the stove, flipping the sizzling bacon.

"I slept great." Connor shrugged.

"I gave you the room with the new mattress." Rebecca looked over her shoulder and winked.

Connor laughed. "Your mom cracks me up."

"Yeah seriously," Emily said, unamused.

"Can you help me with the pancakes, Emily?" her momma asked.

Emily brought down the box of pancake mix and began to follow the instructions on the back. She whipped up the batter and while the griddle heated up, got the syrup and butter out. Soon the breakfast smells of hickory smoked bacon, pancakes, and sweet syrup wafted through the small kitchen.

While the three ate breakfast, Rebecca dressed the

turkey and set it into the oven. She finally sat down to enjoy the now cold breakfast.

"Momma, let me heat this up for you," Emily said, jumping up with a plate of pancakes.

"Thank you, dear."

Emily hit the microwave button and waited.

"What are you guys going to do today?" Rebecca sipped her coffee.

"I'm going to take Connor down to Grandmother's cottage and show him around."

Just then, Walt poked his head into the kitchen. "Football will be on soon, Connor."

Connor smiled.

"I know you don't smoke cigars, but you do watch football, right?" He chuckled, making his belly jiggle a little.

"I don't follow any teams," he said.

Walt huffed then turned around and made his way to the recliner in the other room where he'd be most of the day.

"Daddy, stop picking on Connor, or we're going to leave," Emily yelled.

"Oh, please. Can't he take a little ribbing?" he called out from the other room.

"It's okay, Emily. You don't have to defend me. I can handle him." He nodded toward the living room.

"He's a big teddy bear. He doesn't mean anything," Rebecca said.

"Sometimes his jokes go a bit too far, Momma. You should talk to him about it."

"After thirty-plus years of marriage, I'm not about to change that man. He's who he is, Emily King."

Emily slid out her chair. Leaning over the table, she gathered plates and set them in the sink. "You should get a dishwasher." She began to fill the sink.

"The only time we need a dishwasher is during the holidays. It would take a week of Sundays to fill up one of those machines. We used to have one. When it died, I started washing them by hand."

"Thank goodness you still have a microwave."

"Now, that I can't do without," she snickered.

Emily quickly washed the dishes while Connor dried. Her mom put them away. When the kitchen was tidy, Emily and Connor sneaked out the front door to avoid Walt, leaving Rebecca to get Thanksgiving dinner under the way.

It was a cool morning, even for Texas. Glad for the bulky sweater and jeans, Emily and Connor began their trek two miles down the road. Except for a few birds flying overhead and the squirrel that ran up the tree, the road was lonely and quiet.

As Emily spoke, puffs of white danced in front of her. "I love getting away from all the hustle and bustle of L.A., but not sure I could ever leave it behind permanently. What about you?"

"No, I can't see myself really ever leaving it. I know the idea of a white picket fence is appealing, but it's more a romantic idea, not a realistic one."

"Although with the availability of plane travel, so many places are easy to get to. I mean, look, it only took us two hours to get here."

"Two hours to the airport. Two hours to get here," he said, emphasizing the second here.

"True."

"Anyway, let's enjoy our peaceful holiday and worry about L.A. when we get back." He squeezed her hand.

"Sounds good. Here we are." She motioned up ahead to a small roof that came into view.

"That didn't seem like two miles," he said, picking up the pace.

Sensing his eagerness to see the place, she matched his pace, and soon they were standing on the porch of what used to be her grandparent's cottage.

She pulled out the key from her pocket and dangled it. Inserting it into the lock, she gave it one click and opened the door.

The dust particles hung in the morning sunlight that danced through the blinds. A few pieces of furniture remained in the cottage, giving off an eerie feel.

"I can't believe they haven't cleaned out this place. It's been two years." She patted the white, covered sofa and watched dust billow upward.

"Probably because of the memories," Connor said.

They walked the small cottage room to room in a matter of a few minutes. Two bedrooms and a bath, a small kitchen, and living area. She made her way back through the kitchen and opened the back door where a large, covered deck stained in red, now covered in fallen leaves and other debris, had seen better days.

"Everything needs a refresh. I wonder what their plans are for this property?" Connor asked as they headed back inside.

"Beats me. But maybe they should consider renting it out."

Connor laughed.

Emily furrowed her brows. "What's so funny?"

"Who is going to rent a cottage so far away from civilization? I mean, it's not L.A. where waiting lists are formed, and rent is sky high."

"We are near a town, just not Dallas."

"I must have missed that part while driving here." He bumped shoulders with her.

"That's because Daddy didn't go through it. But tomorrow, I'll take you there."

"I can hardly wait," Connor quipped.

"Okay, I think both Momma and Daddy have rubbed off on you." She ducked her shoulders, then began tickling him in the ribs. He grabbed her hands to make her quit. She lost her balance as they tussled, falling onto the dusty couch, Connor landing on top of her. They stopped laughing.

He reached up and tucked her hair behind her ear. She was aware of the moment, her heavy breathing, the weight of his body on hers. She gulped. "Connor."

He pressed his finger to her lips. "Shh." Then he moved them away and kissed her.

CHAPTER 23

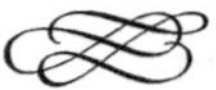

The roasting turkey now consumed the kitchen, replacing the faded memory of the morning's sizzling bacon. Rebecca stood at the counter, chopping and mixing. Emily came up behind her and squeezed her. "How can I help?"

"If you could set the table with Grandmother's china, that would be helpful."

Emily moved to the small dining room that was used only during the holidays. She opened the light-colored oak china cabinet and retrieved the dishes.

"Hey, Momma," she called out as she set the places.

"Uh-huh?"

"Why are you keeping the cottage as is? Do you have any plans for it?"

"We haven't even thought about it."

"It's such a shame to see it whittling away."

A loud noise of a spoon dropping made Emily look up. Had she struck a nerve?

"I mean, it's not doing anyone any good not being lived in."

Silence from the kitchen induced Emily to the fact she did strike a nerve. Holding the silverware in her hand, she crossed over to the adjoining kitchen. "Momma, I know that cottage holds a lot of memories for you. They loved you so much, and you them. My intentions were not to upset you."

Rebecca turned around, wiping her hands on her apron. Leaning up against the counter, she paused as she gathered her words. Emily gave her all the time she needed.

"I don't keep the cottage as a memory. I kept it because I hoped one day my baby girl would come home to stay."

Emily's jaw dropped. "Momma."

"I know. It's a dumb wish. One that'll never come true."

"I didn't say that, Momma. But you do know my home is in L.A. right now."

Rebecca raised her gaze. "Do you mean…"

"I don't know what I mean. I love coming home to you and Daddy, but I love my life in L.A."

"And that's why we haven't done anything with the property." She whirled around and resumed chopping.

Emily turned on her heels and moved back into the dining room, where she finished setting the table.

"Connor probably needs rescuing," Emily said.

"Go ahead. Join them. I'm putting in the dressing and sweet potatoes. Our company should be here in an hour or so. Thought we could play a couple of rounds of cards?"

Emily's ears perked up. "Cards? Gosh, I haven't played cards since the last time I visited."

"What do you guys do for fun out in L.A.? Wait. Never mind. I don't think I want to know."

"Momma!"

Emily poked her head into the living room. Her daddy was snoring in his chair, and Connor looked bored, with glazed eyes from watching football, a sport he didn't even follow.

"I'm surprised you aren't sleeping." She tipped her chin toward Walt.

"Trust me, I've dozed off a few times. The big breakfast, the long walk and to top it off, the boring football game, it's a wonder I'm not flat on my back, mouth wide open snoring along with your daddy."

Emily chuckled. "My relatives will be arriving shortly. Just wanted to give you heads-up. Macy is like Momma, but Tony is the complete opposite of Daddy. You'll probably get along with him fine. Then there are my cousins Bella and Cory. I don't really know Bella's husband. I'd only met him during the rehearsal dinner and wedding. Cory is single, but he may be bringing a friend. I'm not sure."

"If I can handle him"—Connor nodded over to a sleeping Walt—"I can handle anyone." He leaned over and kissed her.

"Mmm. I like your kisses."

"I have more where that came from." He moved in.

"Okay, guys, I'm awake now. You can stop with the kissy face." Walt yawned and stretched, then scratched his head. "I smell food." He released the handle to his recliner, setting the footrest down and stood. "Anyone hungry?" He ran his hand across his belly.

Emily and Connor shook their heads.

"Daddy needs more exercise. Since he retired, he's getting lazy and overweight."

A loud ruckus came from the other room. "They're here."

Connor and Emily moved to the kitchen, where Uncle Tony and Aunt Macy were getting hugs.

"Emily," they called out, rushing to her side and giving her a hug.

"This is my friend Connor. My boyfriend," she said, quickly correcting herself. Emily's gaze moved around them and to the door. "Bella and Cory?"

"They'll be here soon. Bella and Kenny were doing brunch with his parents. Cory is doing who knows what. He knows to be here by four."

The mid-size farmhouse became smaller with the group now packed into the small rooms. Once dinner was served, things moved along at a good pace, but whenever the subject of newlyweds or marriage came up, Emily changed the subject. Why was her momma being so obstinate regarding this?

Bella latched onto her new hubby like a suction cup to a window holding a suncatcher. Sneaking in kisses when they thought no one was looking, and whispering sweet nothings into each other's ear. It was enough to make you nauseated.

"I need some fresh air," Emily said. "You all seem to have this." She tipped her chin toward the assembly line near the sink.

"Sure, honey," Rebecca said, too engrossed in hearing all about Bella's new life as a married woman.

Emily grabbed Connor's hand, and they stepped outside. "I had to get out of there."

"I hear you. It was getting a bit stuffy." He held her hand, making circle patterns on her thumb.

"Stuffy is an understatement. How many times do we have to hear about Bella and what's-his-face."

"Now, Emily. You're not jealous, are you?" He squeezed her hand.

She wouldn't look at him but kept her eyes focused to the woods.

"Emily King. You *are* jealous of them."

She still didn't waver from her stare deep into the woods as far as she could see.

"Don't ever be jealous of anyone. That's what my mom always told me. Be happy for people's successes, be supportive when they fail, and be there for them when they need help picking up the pieces."

Emily pivoted toward him. She blinked a few times. "How profound. Your mother is a genius."

"She was that." He nodded.

"I'm not really jealous of Bella. I just wish I had something great to share."

"You do. You're successful with your own booming photography business. You organized one of the best charity events I've ever been to, and, you have me." He leaned in close.

"I guess when you put it that way..." She raised her chin and posed for the kiss.

He dropped his head a little lower and brushed his lips against hers.

"I love you, Emily. And if I thought for a second you'd accept, I'd ask you to marry me."

Emily drew back. "Are you serious?" She arched her brows.

"Yes, never been more serious about anything. But I know you said you weren't ready for any big commitment like that."

"When did I say that? I must have been delirious."

"You mean you would marry me?"

"I...I...Yes!"

"I don't have a ring or anything. I wasn't expecting to ask you like that."

She grabbed his face with both hands and kissed him firmly on the lips. "I don't have to have a ring. Eventually, I need a ring, but right now, asking me is sweet enough." She leaned in and kissed him again.

"Shall we break the news to your family?"

"Let's wait until the extended family leaves. I don't want to rain on Bella's parade."

"See. You are the bigger person, and another reason I love you so much." He dropped a kiss on her forehead.

"I'm so happy to have everyone over, but so glad to put my feet up," Rebecca said, plopping down into her recliner.

"You outdid yourself again this year, Momma."

"That you did, honey," Walt said. "That second piece of pie did me in." He patted his belly.

"Dad, have you thought about getting some exercise?"

Walt showed his dissatisfaction by making a grumpy sound.

"Start off slow. You and Momma take a walk after dinner each night. It's addictive," Emily sang.

"Maybe," Walt said.

"Think about it, because I want you and Momma around for a long time. You know, to share in my happiness, my wedding day, and grandchildren."

"Okay, hon. I'll think about it."

Emily knitted her brows.

"Did you hear what I said? Weddings and grandchildren?"

Rebecca had had her eyes closed, resting. They flew open, and she rose straight out of her chair. "Weddings! Grandchildren!"

"Yes, Connor has asked me to marry him."

Rebecca ran over to them and wrapped her arms around them both. "I'm so happy for you two. Did you hear that, Walt? A wedding!"

"Rebecca, I heard. And my wallet cried."

"Oh, Daddy!"

"Kidding. So, when's the date?"

"I don't know. He just asked me." She looked to Connor for a response.

"I don't know. Maybe in the spring?"

"Spring weddings are so pretty," Rebecca said, her eyes pooling with tears.

"Momma, don't start crying now. You have to save those tears for the big day."

"Connor Stone, welcome to the family," Walt said.

"What? No jokes about welcoming him to the family?" Emily offered her dad a puzzled look.

"Well, I was going to say something like, her dowry is two hens and a cow, or show me your bank account so I can see if you're worthy of our daughter, but I can tell by the smile on your face he's more than worthy, and I don't need any more farm animals to care for." Walt chuckled.

"Love you, Daddy."

"Love you, too, Emily."

CHAPTER 24

"You look so beautiful," Connor said, eyeing her up and down.

"Thank you. You look rather dashing yourself."

She slid in as he held the door open.

With one hand on the steering wheel and one holding her hand, they made small talk as he weaved in and out of the heavy L.A. traffic.

"Where are we going? You never told me."

"It's a surprise."

"I love surprises."

But when he drove up in front of the restaurant, the surprise was over.

"La Joliesse!". Connor handed his keys over to the valet.

They held hands across the small table in the corner.

"I always thought when I asked the woman of my dreams to marry me, it would be somewhere romantic."

"It was special, Connor. I loved the way it happened."

"I also thought I would have a ring." He let go of her hand and pulled out a ring from his pocket.

Her hand flew to her mouth.

He popped open the black velvet box. Emily couldn't take her eyes off the gleaming diamonds.

"It's so beautiful," she said, blinking back the tears.

He removed the ring and held it between his thumb and finger. "Emily King, the love of my life, will you marry me?"

"Yes!"

He slid the ring on her finger, and lifting her hand to his mouth, gingerly kissed her hand. "I love you."

"Connor, I'm so happy right now I can't even think straight."

"Let's set a date."

"Okay," she said, clearly rattled. She grabbed her phone and scrolled to the calendar. "How about May twelfth. It's a Saturday, and it's Mother's Day weekend. Perfect time for a wedding in Texas."

"Texas?"

"Yeah, so my parents and family can be there." She tilted her head, keeping her gaze steady on his.

"They could fly out here, couldn't they? I have tons of friends here."

"True, but they could also fly to Texas. It's not like they don't have the money." She chuckled, trying to keep all nervousness out of her voice.

"I guess we should have discussed all of that before we got so serious," Connor said, sitting back into his seat.

"That's a minor detail of where the wedding will be. I'm sure we can work it out," Emily said, trying to get things back on track.

"Are you sure? Because if it's going to get all complicated, we could fly to Vegas."

"My momma would never forgive me if we ran off to Vegas, Connor."

"How about two ceremonies?"

Emily brushed off his idea with a wave of her hand. "I think that's overkill. I'll call Momma tonight and see what she thinks about getting my aunt and uncle, two cousins and their significant others on a plane to California. There's only eight of them. We have too many friends and business associates to even count."

THE NEXT FEW months dragged as winter approached Southern California. Wet and fog hit the area, making the months feel even longer. But planning the wedding kept Emily busy, and it was a good thing because the photography business had also slowed down. She'd already put the feelers out that Sara Beth would be handling some of the load the closer it got to the wedding.

After searching for the best venue to have the wedding, Connor and Emily decided to hold it at a beautiful winery with views of Malibu Canyon and the nest of the awesome mountain range. When they toured it, it was raining, but they both could visualize how beautiful it would be come springtime.

And for music, they both agreed Jay's Garage Band would perform, and for the food, none other than La Joliesse. The winery would provide tables, chairs, and even the wine! The cake was the next thing to check off.

After Emily looked at several pictures online of design

ideas, Margo's gourmet dog biscuits entered her mind. She may be the baker of dog treats, but she was a whiz in the kitchen, and when Emily shared a sample of the wedding invitation, she promised to design the cake using lavender flowers and ribbon, and instead of the traditional bride and groom topper, two doves holding wedding bands.

Once all the wedding details were hashed out, Emily took a breather and concentrated on her photography business. It was beginning to ramp up with graduation and wedding photos. Sara Beth helped her out so much, and Emily told her each and every day how blessed she was to find her. But nothing made her happier than when Sara Beth told her the good news.

"I have a prearranged visit with my children!"

"I'm so happy for you. What changed his mind, do you suppose?"

Emily hadn't told her about her little chat with him, and it had been a few months since they had the talk, surely, he came to the conclusion on his own.

"I don't really know, or care, I'm just glad he decided to. I'm so anxious, though. Will they be kind to me, will they open up to me, will they embrace me."

"Of course, they will. They are your babies."

EMILY WAITED on pins and needles for Sara Beth to get back from her visit with her children. Poor Sara Beth was shaking so badly her teeth chattered.

When the door flew open, and Emily was almost blinded by the sparkle in her eyes, she knew the visit had gone well. Sara Beth ran up and hugged her as she choked back her emotions.

"It's okay, Sara Beth. It's okay," Emily said, holding her.

"They accepted me with open arms," she said, wiping the tears.

"I told you they would."

"Their daddy's been doing a decent job holding them all together. I'll give him that much."

Emily tried to hide her smirk. Glad he did that at least, she mused.

"When do you see them again?"

"Soon. We're planning a trip to the happiest place on earth!"

"Well, Sara Beth, it will be hard to beat this place, at this moment, but I get you. They'll have fun on the rides." She patted her arm. "I'm so happy it's all working out for you."

"I told the girls that Mommy was wrong for what she did and paid the ultimate price. And that if I learned anything while locked up, it was how precious my family is to me. I told them several times each day I thought about them. Wondered what they were doing, how they were getting along." She began to cry again.

"What did they say?"

"They said they've been talking to the school counselor and it has helped ease the pain and shame they've been carrying around. They said they wanted to visit me, but their father wouldn't let them. I could have talked bad about his decision, but instead, I took the high road and told them he was just sparing them more hurt."

"That a girl. See. I knew there was a pot of gold at the

end of the rainbow. Things will get better. One step at a time. Baby steps."

"Baby steps," Sara Beth echoed.

"Let's get to work. We have high school graduation photos, and you know those kids can be wild."

"You got it, boss. Emily?"

Emily whirled around, holding a stuffed bear they'd used in an earlier session. "Yes?"

"Thank you for giving me a chance. Thanks for being my friend."

Emily flashed a smile. "You're a wonderful photographer and a human being. Let's get to work before I start bawling too." She tossed the bear into the bin with the other stuffed animals. She pulled the blue velvet material out from the storage place and started to unroll it. She pitched the one end to Sara Beth. "Here, help me lay this out."

They snapped the material open, draping it across the various cubes where the kids would be sitting and standing. Sara pulled down the soft white background screen. Noise from the other side of the door from boisterous teens let them both know their first group had arrived.

Emily waved them in. A tall, gangly boy with spiked hair, a dark-haired girl with nose piercings, and another girl with rounded hips and purple hair came in, each of them jostling one another and carrying on with high-pitched bantering.

"Those were the days, huh?" Emily whispered to Sara Beth.

"I know. And I have girls who'll grow up to be teens. Help me," she murmured.

Emily laughed. "Okay, guys. Listen up so we won't be here all day."

"This is dope," the kid with the spiked hair said.

Emily had been around enough to know dope meant sweet and sweet meant cool. Cool. Now that was a word worth repeating. She shrugged then peered into the lens. "Say cheese."

CHAPTER 25

"I can't believe this day is finally here," Emily said, shaking uncontrollably.

"You've got this," Kayla said.

"I have you to thank, ya know." Emily's eyes began to mist.

"I just introduced you two. You guys made it happen." She reached for Emily's hands.

"I'm about to become Emily Stone." She squeezed her best friends' hands.

"I'm so happy to have you as my best friend and soon, sister."

"Sister. I always wanted a sister."

"I hear the music. Are you ready?"

"I've been ready for a while. Let's get this show on the road!"

"Parents. Can I get your attention? Walt. It's time." Kayla motioned for him to come over.

Rebecca and Walt came rushing over.

"You look absolutely radiant," Rebecca said.

"My little girl," Walt said, blinking back tears.

"They just repeated the chorus. Get going you two," Kayla ordered in her best maid of honor voice.

She ran out the door of the little cottage. Rebecca followed her to take her seat in the front row.

Walt lifted his arm, Emily looped her arm with his, and trying their best to ward off the flood of emotions that were hitting them both, in time to the music, they stepped their way to the arbor laced in beautiful lavender and yellow flowers, where Connor, the man of her dreams, stood by.

IN THE DISTANCE echoing off the nestled mountains of the gorgeous canyon, Jay's Garage Band played on.

"Well, Mrs. Stone. How does it feel?" He held her by the waist as they swayed to the music.

"It feels great. How about you?"

"I'm floating on clouds," Connor said, his gaze warm and alluring.

"I can't even put it into words. I know things are about to get crazy for us, with the premiere of your movies and all, but after things die down, we have to get away. I don't care where, but somewhere peaceful." She laid her head on his chest, and they shuffled their feet to the music.

"I can only think of one place so peaceful." Connor lifted her chin with his finger.

Her face relaxed as she tried to guess this place. "Where is that at?"

"At your grandparents' cottage."

EPILOGUE

The sounds of all the cameras clicking and people shoving mics in his face drove her insane. Did they not respect anyone's privacy at all? She held on to his hand as he pushed his way through the crowd. "Connor Stone," they yelled. She ducked her head as she bulldozed her way in, following close behind him. Finally, they rounded a corner where a black limousine waited for them.

He threw open the door and quickly ushered her in, sliding in and pulling the door behind. "Quick, let's get the heck out here," Connor said to the driver.

"Yes, sir. Where to?"

"Airport. We have a flight to catch to Texas."

"Congratulations, Connor," Walt and Rebecca said in unison.

"Thank you. It's sort of overwhelming. One minute

I'm performing on stage and the next, I'm making not one, but two movies."

"And a hit movie at that," Emily said, snuggled close to his body.

"It was a fluke." He was humble as the day was long.

"Fluke! No way. You were so good in that movie," Rebecca said. "I couldn't take my eyes off of you, and your lines, spoken like a true professional."

"Okay, now you guys are going to make me turn red."

"Hate to tell you this, Connor, but you've already turned every shade of red," Walt said, chuckling.

"What's next for you?" Rebecca asked.

"He's doing a live interview on a talk show," Emily said breathlessly.

"You're going places, kid." Walt chortled.

"WHAT?"

He took the white rag he held in his hand and wiped the paint from her nose. She giggled.

"I love you, Mrs. Stone." He kissed the spot he'd erased of paint.

"Love you too. I think it looks great." She turned around, spooning him. He wrapped his arms around her.

"I think it looks better than great." His gaze moved up and down the recently painted walls. A mixture between a beige and a gray to match the gray-toned flooring they'd installed.

"Who would have ever thought the big movie star Connor Stone could be so great with his hands."

He whirled her around and held her tight. "I could say

something about that, but I'll save it for later." He dropped a kiss to her mouth.

A big sigh escaped her lips as she moved about the room, touching the new pieces of furniture they'd painstakingly put together, the antique ones left behind they'd sanded and stained, giving the cottage the farmhouse look they both desired. "A place of our own when we want to get away from it all." She drew in her bottom lip. "A place for the children to play when visiting Grandma and Grandpa."

"Are you saying what I think you're saying?"

She nodded.

He picked her up, twirling her around and around. Daisy started barking, adding to the chaos. "Our own little Emily or Connor," he said, plopping down on the sofa and taking her down with him.

"Yep. Our only little mini-me's." She giggled.

"It's going to be hard with my crazy schedule, but I promise to be the best dad ever."

"I'll bring them to the studio with me. It'll all work out. You'll see." She rested her hand on his leg.

"I can't wait to see the look on Walt's face."

"Me, either." Nestling her head in the crux of his shoulder, they propped their feet up on the coffee table, taking in the silence of their beautiful moment.

ABOUT THE AUTHOR

A USA Today bestselling author, Debbie writes sweet contemporary romance and women's fiction. She lives in South Carolina with her husband and one slightly spoiled silky wire dachshund who they affectionately call Princess Viola. She loves to hike, work in the garden, and on most sunny days you can find her enjoying her backyard. She's an avid supporter of animal rescue, and as such, pledges to happily donate a percentage of all book sales to local and national rescue organizations. When you purchase any of her books, you're also helping animals.

To find out more about Debbie, check out her website at: https://www.authordebbiewhite.com